ALL THAT IS IN THE EARTH

ANDREW KNIGHTON

LUNA NOVELLA #24

Text Copyright © 2026 Andrew Knighton
Cover © 2026 Jay Johnstone

Editorial Team: Francesca T Barbini, Racheal Kizza
Typesetting: Francesca T Barbini
First published by Luna Press Publishing, Edinburgh, 2026

A CIP catalogue record is available from the British Library

www.lunapresspublishing.com
ISBN-13: 978-1-915556-67-7

For Dan Prebble,
who has sharpened many of my bluntest ideas and
helped me create the setting for this book.

Contents

Chapter One

Clifford didn't cry. Despite the pain and the shock that shook his body. Despite the dizziness so intense he wanted to puke himself unconscious. Despite the mile-long trail of destruction his shuttle had torn through the emerald beauty of hell, blades of broken ship's hull scything through trees, friction and vented fuel scorching all life from its wake. Despite the fact that his friends and colleagues were dead. Despite the fact that he was as good as dead too.

He didn't cry because to cry would be to acknowledge the chasm that had opened inside his mind, the unfathomable certainty of oblivion. He was too scared to cry, to run, to do anything except stare out through his helmet and the window beyond, into the heat haze and the smoke drifting out across a planet where only the dead dwelt. He prayed to a god he'd never believed in, and he stared.

In orbit, everything had been stillness, the motion of the stars too slow to register in a sentient mind, the clouds that swirled across the face of Abaddon moving at a hypnotic pace. The vessels in orbit were all part of the blockade, gleaming tubes and tori bristling with weaponry and staffed with specialist observers, their mission to contain. Abaddon had no shuttles or elevators running to the surface, and the only ships passing through the area stopped off station while they unloaded supplies. He had seen more motion in a bare field on a parched summer's day.

Down here, though, things were different. Lush leaves rustled, grasses shimmered, trees a hundred times taller than Clifford swayed to the music of the wind. In the blackened trail he'd ripped through that life, chunks of dirt and debris shifted, while flames crawled with flickering brightness into the dryer stands of undergrowth. Oily smoke trickled upward, coalesced into a column, spread into a grey smear against which birds whirled. The whole world seemed so alive, which made it all the more bitter to know that he was dead.

A hollow gaped inside his heart. Every nerve around it was raw, aching, longing for the life he had lost. It wasn't even dread, that was too concrete a word for what he faced. To dread something you had to be able to imagine it, and Clifford had no idea how death would feel. All he knew was life, and the desperate desire not to lose that.

The glass of his helmet clinked against the glass of the window as he tried to get a better view. The shuttle was tipped on its side, the door halfway horizontal, everything thrown into angles that added to his disorientation. His world had twisted off its axis.

Something was moving at the edge of the forest. Perhaps it would eat his body once this was over. The Scattered Brethren believed that there was hope in returning to the cycle of life, becoming part of another living thing, but Clifford had never found comfort in mysticism. Death was death. The mind ended with the body and no illusions could shelter him from that.

The safety of the shuttle was one of those illusions now. It had saved him from the destruction of Eldwise Station, carried him clear of the blasts rocking the station and ahead of the power plant's cataclysmic collapse. But even before debris pierced his engines, he'd known that he was on the wrong course, the autopilot carrying him down into the quarantine zone, not up and away. Then there had been vibrations, smoke, screeching, and an atmospheric entry in which he'd only just kept the shuttle flying straight. Now, as he pressed his helmet against the glass, he saw a crack.

Until then, there had been hope, however distant, not for a whole life but for a few more days, clinging on in the shuttle, reading books, writing notes for his family in case they were ever retrieved, or more likely for posterity, to be found in thousands of years once Abaddon was somehow made clean. But if the seal of the shuttle was broken, then the planet's air was in. He only had as long as his suit's oxygen supply lasted.

He might as well make the most of that. What better way to spend these final moments than to finally touch the dirt of Abaddon, after watching it for so long from afar?

With a trembling hand, he disabled the door lock. In his other hand, he held his sampling kit, the one Aunt Prein had bought him for his eighteenth birthday. The only personal possession he'd brought to Eldwise Station, and for some reason the only possession he'd taken on fleeing the station, except for a single photo of his parents. Other people might have grabbed emergency supplies or a gun, but some panicked part of his mind had valued that case more than life itself. So now, as the door hissed open and the wind blew in, he climbed over the lip of the twisted, tilted doorway and slid down the outside of the shuttle with that sampling kit in his hand.

The moment his boots touched the ground, he knew that it was good dirt. It gave beneath his weight, the softness of soil that was well watered and ventilated, in which millions of micro-organisms processed organic matter in a constant cycle. Old leaves became food for arthropods and worms, whose leavings provided for fungi and bacteria, which brought nutrients to the roots of plants, whose leaves fell once more. Life continued, unbreakable, until people interfered with their pesticides and their feeds. With their shattering explosions against the black of space.

He sank to his knees, clutching the sampling kit to his chest, the polished brown metal of the box against the blue of his spacesuit. He wanted to cry, but the tears were weighed beneath the unfathomable horror of the moment. How could the prospect of nothing become something so huge?

Rasping, choking gasps burst from him. He wanted to tear off the helmet, to feel the wind on his face, but he couldn't bear to bring the end closer just for the moment's relief.

Something moved at the edge of the destruction, where living trees towered over the fallen ones. Was that a glimpse of a pale and thick-veined body, like the pictures from his training? Somehow, the concrete fear of being devoured wasn't so bad as abstract oblivion. The tears flowed and he sagged over his kit. It was almost a relief when the glass started steaming up.

Then came a rumble that grew to a roar, and for a terrible moment he was back in the station's smoke-filled launch bay.

A vehicle burst from the forest, mismatched chassis plates gleaming, a plough on the front flinging fallen logs aside. It bucked and growled across the rutted dirt and swung to a halt by the shuttle, its tracks tossing clods of dirt across Clifford.

An armoured hatch opened, and a woman leaped out. She was green-skinned, wearing solid boots, red sweatpants, and a knitted sweater unravelling at the elbows. A slouched woollen hat covered most of her head.

"If you want to live, give me a hand," she said, raising her voice over the idling of her armoured truck.

Clifford stared at her. "We're already dead."

"One of those, huh?" She strode past Clifford, a crowbar in her hand. "In that case, what have you got?"

"I... What?" Clifford raised his head.

"Food, medicine, water purifiers?" She grabbed the edge of the shuttle hatch and hauled herself in. "What did you bring with you?"

"I didn't... I wasn't..." Clifford pushed himself to his feet. "What are you doing?"

"What do you think I'm doing?" The woman's voice echoed out of the craft. It was followed a moment later by a tool kit and two spare space suits. "Oxygen packs. Nice." Her head appeared around the edge of the buckled door frame. "Which feudality are you from?"

"How do you..."

"Blaster Corp don't use these shuttle frames for its own ships, and you obviously ain't Pack. Your skin's wrong for one of my people, Ossians barely exist, I could go on. You're clearly feudality, so which one?"

"I serve the Earldom of Wecks."

"Wecks, huh?" She disappeared back inside. "Probably good battery packs, then, but the wiring won't be any use."

There was a creak and a crack, then components from the shuttle's interior started flying out the door.

"You can't take that!" Clifford hurried over.

"Why not?" The innards of a food printer hurtled past his head.

"Because it doesn't belong to you!"

"You said you're dead, so it can't be yours." She appeared at the hatch, looked around the jungle, then ducked back inside. "Your feudality won't come for a shuttle that's crossed the quarantine line. So, by God's will, I'm claiming it for myself."

"It belongs to the Earl, and it's station equipment, and Commander Dommel will have me fined if..."

His voice trailed off. Dommel was dead. Everyone on the station was. Clifford had looked back as he left, seen two other shuttles leave the bay only to be shattered in the blast. There was no station, no commander, no chain of loyal links connecting him to the Earl of Wecks. He didn't even know what had sundered them, why the station had so suddenly and cataclysmically been ripped apart. He was adrift.

Clifford wrung his hands. He wanted to run screaming into the jungle, to face the end that was coming, to have certainty. But it was a final certainty, a darkness emptier than space itself.

A touch made Clifford jump, snapping him back into his body, in the jungle, at the door of the wreck. The woman's bare fingers were resting on the arm of his suit. Her smile was soft and sorrowful.

"I've been there," she said. "We all have. But right now, you've got two choices." She pulled herself up to straddle the tilted lip of the doorway and dragged the pilot's seat up. "Either you help me load Breda and get out of here, or you wait around for them."

She tossed the seat into her scavenged pile and pointed toward the edge of the forest.

Creatures were emerging. Some of them were a fraction of Clifford's height, some twice as tall as him; a few on two legs but most on four or six; some with clusters of feathers, others with tufts of fur, all with bald patches where their swollen flesh had pushed through protective and decorative layers. That flesh, like all of their flesh, was pale and sagging, shot through with thick, dark veins. The head of one horse-like creature trembled and a section of its neck slid off, breaking into chunks and dust as it fell, but the beast didn't collapse. Instead, with awkward, uneven steps it joined the other creatures heading across the broken ground, their dead bodies held together by the thing that was devouring them, that drove them after flesh the disease could consume instead of their own—the chalk rot.

Clifford stared at his future: to be devoured by them or become one of them, did it matter? Abaddon was the swarm and the swarm was Abaddon. Clifford's own days were at an end.

The woman was on the move again, lurching back and forth between the shuttle and her misshapen vehicle, carrying her scavengings with her. Birds had started to settle, pecking curiously at the hull of the shuttle and more productively at the dirt.

"Seriously," she snapped. "Now's your chance to live, so take it."

"I'm already dead." Clifford couldn't take his eyes off the twisted creatures advancing on them. "The moment I open my suit, I'm infected. Why resist?"

"Your suit's already open." She pointed at his leg. "You feeling dead yet?"

There was a ragged gash in the calf of Clifford's suit, and a cool breeze on his skin that he hadn't let himself notice. A flash of blue on a jutting shuttle strut told him that he'd done this as he scrambled down. How could he be such an idiot?

He sobbed again. Could he feel the chalk rot in his chest already, a pain like tiny hooks in his lungs?

"Snap out of it." She dragged the seat through the dirt. "They get faster as they get closer."

"But I..." His view was steaming up. He wrenched off his helmet and flung it down, letting the wind brush his skin, the tears flow free. One last moment of living.

"Careful with that!" The woman grabbed the helmet and carried it away. "That suit still has its uses."

"What uses?" Clifford screamed, scattering the birds. "This is Abaddon! No one leaves! No one lives! If we're not infected then we'll be eaten, so what's the point of any of it?"

The woman was stronger than she looked. Her slap knocked Clifford's head to one side and left his cheek stinging.

"Sorry," she said. "I can't abide violence, but God didn't put us here to wallow."

"This is pointless," he whispered. "Sooner or later, we're dead."

"So is everyone. Life is what you do between now and then."

"So go live. Let me meet my fate."

Her gaze flitted from him to her truck to the swarm of pale bodies coming closer by the minute.

"If I wasn't an honest woman, I'd make up some rank for myself, try to order you into obeying. But this ain't the feudality, and that ain't my way. I will tell you that there are other folks on this planet, people who've survived for years, despite what they tell you out there. You look like a useful guy, and the more useful guys we have, the better everyone's chance to live. So, you and I can grab one last load and get into Breda, or I can drag you inside and we get away with less. But either way, you're coming with me."

Maybe it was the authority in her voice; maybe it was the sense of duty that came with knowing others needed him; maybe some part of Clifford hadn't quite given up on living. He didn't know what it was, but his legs moved him towards the shuttle door.

"There's a gun rack in the back," he said.

"No guns. They only cause trouble."

"But the swarm—"

"Can't run as fast as us."

They were both in, grabbing whatever lay around: communicators, battery packs, a loose control board. Then they were out, down the outside of the shuttle and back toward the truck, while the swarm picked up speed, warped bodies rustling as they ran. As he passed his sampling kit, Clifford shoved the control board under his arm and picked up the metal case. What was a soil scientist without his sample jars?

He tripped at the door of the truck and stumbled into its roaring innards.

"Close the door," the woman shouted as she took the driver's seat. "Quick, they're almost here!"

Clifford grabbed the handle. One of the swarm, a dog-shaped thing as high as his waist, was dashing across the churned dirt. Clifford's heart hammered as he heaved on the handle. The creature leaped, claw outstretched. With a thud, the door ploughed through the pale and swollen flesh of the creature's leg, but there was no howl of pain. Then something in the door hissed, motors kicking in. A sickening crunch and the door locked, leaving Clifford staring at a severed paw.

The world around him rumbled as they drove away.

Chapter Two

The truck rumbled through the jungle, jolting over broken ground and shuddering as it smashed trees aside. There were rustles and hisses, the sounds of branches and undergrowth brushing the flanks as they passed. The air in the truck smelled of ethanol, crushed leaves, and the blood oozing from the severed paw.

Clifford pressed himself into a corner, head in his hands, staring at the paw. A few seconds slower with the door and that thing would have had him. The air was warm, but his fingers felt cold, and his chest tingled. That must be the chalk rot, the thing that had consumed the beast and that would kill him. He clutched his sampling kit tight.

"Get up here," the woman shouted. "Tell me what you think of these clouds."

Clifford took a breath. It didn't hurt like he expected; if anything, the tingling sensation was fading. So why did he feel tears welling?

There was a splash of blood on his spacesuit, and something white. White like the rotting, crumbling flesh of the swarm. White like the disease.

In a panic, Clifford tore himself out of the suit and flung it across the hold.

"The chalk rot, it's in here!"

He grabbed a tube of sanitiser off his belt, slathered it across his hands and rubbed them together, fingers wrenching and twisting in his panicked attempt to scour the foreign touch from his skin.

"Of course it's in here," the woman replied. "The whole planet's thick with it."

"You don't understand, it's—"

"Get up here. I didn't save your life so you could sit on your ass."

There was a short ladder up from the cargo space. Clifford wiped the last of the sanitiser onto a rag then climbed the thick, smooth rungs and hauled himself through a hatch in the wall, into the cab.

The woman sat at the vehicle's controls, one hand on a control yoke, the other fishing around in a tin can clipped onto the dash. She took a couple of dried insects from the tin and tossed them into her mouth, then pointed out the windscreen and up.

"You know much about clouds?" she asked.

Clifford took the seat beside her and looked at where she was pointing. Through the smeared glass and gaps in the jungle canopy, he caught glimpses of thick cloud banks, white and grey, roiling across the sky.

"Cumulonimbus," he said. "Tall ones, heading..."

He glanced across the controls but couldn't see anything navigational.

"West," the woman said.

"Heading west. If we keep going like this, we're going to end up under a storm."

"That's the plan." She tapped the tin of insects. "Help yourself."

Clifford peered inside. His stomach was still churning from the crash, and the thought of eating made him feel sick. Could he refuse, or would that be impolite? What was the etiquette for food in a plague zone?

That thought made him laugh, a mad, jagged sound he'd never heard before, and its edges cut so hard that tears fell. Ashamed, he turned his head away, shoulders hunched to withstand her judgement. The piercing scent of sanitiser clung to his hands.

"Not to your tastes, huh?" She shrugged. "That's cool. My name's Emieke Solvesdin, by the way. Technically Doctor Solvesdin, but you can call me Emi."

A doctor. That made it worse.

"My name is Clifford Foster."

"Cliff, huh?"

The clipped name, unfamiliar and far too familiar, tweaked one more raw nerve among the many running through Clifford. He wished that he was allowed to correct a social superior.

"I prefer Clifford," he said, trying not to sound demanding.

"Really?" Doctor Solvesdin shrugged. "What do you do, *Clifford*, when you ain't being marooned?"

It was a curious choice of words. Wasn't marooning something the Red Blade did when they kicked a member out of their crew? He hadn't been left here by pirates, and certainly not by his own people.

The truck bucked as they drove across the protruding roots of a vast tree, its bark a warm bronze. Clifford grabbed the straps attached to his seat and buckled himself in.

"I'm a soil scientist," he said. "I'm doing research toward a doctorate in unusual rhizospheric systems."

"A researcher, huh? I thought you were something practical, like a technician."

"Certainly not."

"Then why are you dressed like that?"

She gestured at his well-kept overalls, the belt of shiny tools, and the cap thrust through that belt. Clifford shrank into himself, feeling excruciatingly alive. He wished he had the imagination for anything other than the truth.

"I thought it looked cool." His cheeks flushed with heat.

"And they let you get away with that?" Doctor Solvesdin asked. "I thought that feudality scholars had to wear suits."

"Being on an Abaddon orbital counts as field work." He lowered his breath to a mutter. "Technically."

She laughed. "No need to feel embarrassed: no one here cares how you dress; we've got more pressing concerns. Speaking of which..." She pointed to a lever on the ceiling. "Be a good guy and check that we've lost the swarm, will you?"

Clifford pulled the lever down and a viewing lens followed, sliding out of the ceiling. Clacking sounds unfolded above.

Peering into the lens, Clifford saw the jungle behind them, the view surprisingly steady given the movements of the truck. There was some sort of spring suspension in there, and a clever pivot that let the lens rotate around Clifford's head as he turned, giving him a hundred-and-eighty degree view. Everything was greens and browns, or the colourful splashes of flowers, their brightness dimmed under thickening clouds. No sign of the stumbling shapes that had menaced the crash site.

"I don't see any swarm," he said. "Though given the density of the foliage, there is room for error."

"You can just say all clear. Sometimes, speed matters more than precision."

Clifford slid the viewer back into the ceiling and bowed his head. In his work, precision was everything, but it wasn't his place to correct a doctor. "I'll remember that."

There was a sharp tapping sound, then another. Doctor Solvesdin turned a dial, and wipers swished back and forth across the windscreen, just as the rain started in force.

"What brings a soil scientist to Abaddon?" she asked, raising her voice over the noise.

"As I said, my research."

"Plenty of other places you can study soil."

"I hoped to find something more."

"Of course you did." She laughed. "Let me guess, your duchy wants to understand the ecosystem that spawned chalk rot."

"How did you know?"

"Why do you think so many folks are helping with the blockade?"

"To stop the disease escaping again."

"Sure, yes, but also to poke at it, to learn something no one else knows."

"The treaty says they can't do that." He heard the indignation in his voice, even as he realised the hypocrisy. His cheeks grew even warmer.

"Funny how many ways they find of working around that. What was yours?"

He shouldn't be sharing information, but he had to answer a superior, and that conflict tightened Clifford's insides. Fortunately, for once, the solution was easy: what did it matter when they were both dead?

"Drones bring samples up to satellites below the blockade, with their own testing systems. They're kept strictly separate, no direct contact with our station, to maintain the quarantine." That last part wasn't technically correct. The drones had broken the letter of the law, but Clifford had convinced himself that it was acceptable. The programme kept within the spirit of the rules, and in the long term, wouldn't the knowledge gained help keep people safe? "My first sample was arriving today."

"Ah." She patted his leg. "Sorry about that. You want to tell me more about what happened?"

For a terrible moment, Clifford was back aboard the station. Failing lights. Blaring alarms. Shuddering decks. The wrenching scream as metal tore.

He shook his head, barely more than a shudder. It wasn't as if he understood. Just explosions, and then...

The thunder of rain on their roof intensified. Doctor Solvesdin looked at a sensor that Clifford didn't recognise.

"Better stop for a bit."

The truck eased to a halt, caught between the roots of one of the vast trees. The doctor turned off the engine and turned to face Clifford, her seat rotating with her.

"It ain't so bad down here," she said. "Once you get used to it."

"How can that possibly be?" He stared out into a forest battered by the rain. There was a hypnotic beauty to the movements of the emerald leaves. "Infection rates for the chalk rot run at twenty-two percent per day for any human variant sharing its biosystem, ninety-four percent following contact with an infected body, and fatality rates are ninety-seven point six percent over twenty days."

"That depends on how you define fatality."

Doctor Solvesdin smiled. Clifford didn't.

"Becoming one of those things is hardly life."

"As a medical professional, I'd have to agree with you, though as a woman of faith, that's a more complex question. But there's something else you're missing."

She pointed at the lever on the ceiling, the one attached to the viewing lens.

"I made that adaptation myself. Overhauled Breda's engines too. Installed new seats, replaced the wheels, fixed the exhaust. Winds know, there's barely an original bit of the old girl left. Could I have done that with only twenty days until death?"

Clifford frowned. "You did it down here?"

"Noone drives trucks like Breda out in the universe." She laughed. "I made all those changes and more."

"How long..."

"Have I been down here? Five years and change."

"But that's..." Clifford's voice rose like a child's. "Doctor Solvesdin, you must be mistaken."

"You came here looking for something new, didn't you?"

"You have a cure?" His pulse quickened. In spite of the rain thundering down, the jungle around them seemed brighter.

"Not a cure, exactly, but a way to survive. A medicine that fends off the chalk rot, so long as you keep taking it."

"We're not..."

"Dead?" She laughed. "Last time I checked, I wasn't a corpse."

Some giddy part of Clifford wanted to make a joke about green being the colour of rot, but that was the sort of comment Aunt Prein would make, and you didn't say such things outside of small towns. At least, not to people's faces.

"I'm not dead?" he asked, fighting back laughter that was as much incredulity as relief.

"Not yet."

He let himself laugh, so long and hard that his chest ached and the tears ran again. Outside, the rain was easing, but it was no quieter inside the cab.

"Hm." The doctor raised an eyebrow almost up to her woollen cap. "Might need to get you a sedative."

"No, no." Clifford waved a hand and forced himself to stillness, sitting up straight in his seat. "I'll pull myself together."

"No need for that. You've been through a lot, better to go with it. Besides, we'll be here a while." She reached under her seat, pulled out a box the size of her hand, and took out a syringe full of milky purple liquid. "Show me your arm."

"That's it?" Clifford asked as he rolled up his sleeve. "The cure?"

"Like I said, not a cure, but it'll hold off the infection, once it gets inside you." She jabbed the needle into his upper arm and depressed the plunger. Clifford felt a slight ache as she drew the needle out. "All done. You're safe from whatever's in the air, just don't get bitten or clawed by anything infected, there are limits to what this can do." She put the syringe back into the box. "And we're running low, which is why we need the rain."

"Why would that—"

There was a tap on the window and Clifford jerked around, shoulders jolting against his harness. A face stared in, and for an awful moment he thought that it was one of the swarm. Then he realised that the paleness wasn't dead flesh but light-toned human skin, framed by a hood of water-proofed camo-pattern cloth, its expression stern. Reality didn't make Clifford's heart race any less.

Doctor Solvesdin laughed.

"She's a friend," she said. "Pretty much everyone is, down here in the dirt, at least until the rot gets hold of them. Go ahead and wind the window down."

Clifford found a mechanical handle and wrenched it in circles until the glass was halfway down. A breeze blew in, and with it the clear, refreshing scent of rain. The drops brushing his cheek, his first real weather after months on transport ships and orbital stations, was like a message from home, a memory of his mother standing under an apple tree, watching spring shoots unfurl in the fields. His hand went to his pocket, and he curled himself around that memory, something familiar in a universe turned on its head.

"Captain Joom Tork," the doctor said. "This here is Clifford."

"Clifford Foster," Clifford said, lowering the window further so that he could hold out his hand. He'd been around enough soldiers to know that he, a civilian, shouldn't salute. "Honoured to meet you, Captain."

"Sure." Tork didn't even look at the hand. "Looks like the BDS is over, Doc. You and the new lad want to join us for some grub?"

"That would be mighty fine, thank you."

"Two BFTs that way." Tork pointed through the thinning rain. "Bring your kit. Marel's been playing with the biome again."

Tork strode away, her camouflage poncho disappearing into the undergrowth.

"What's a BDS?" Clifford asked.

"Big Damn Storm." The doctor unfastened her straps and opened her door.

"And a BFT?"

"Big Forest Tree, apparently, though I suspect they've changed the F for me. These folks love a good acronym, even when it's no quicker to say." She climbed out of the cab. "Come on, I'll make the introductions."

Solvesdin pulled a bag from under her seat, then set off through the trees. Clifford followed. Though the rain had got lighter, it only took a few steps for the refreshing reminder of home to become a damp seeping through his clothes.

Two trees away proved a longer walk than back home. The undergrowth here was bigger than the trees he'd climbed as a kid, while the trunks of the trees themselves were wide as houses, with surface roots as broad as tractors. Though he'd left his sampling kit on board Breda, Clifford couldn't resist stopping to press his fingers into the dirt around one of those roots, feeling its consistency, soaking up its soft scent. Good soil, no doubt about that.

A thin synthetic membrane had been stretched between some of the sturdier undergrowth, forming a spacious shelter. Beyond that was a military transport, sleeker than Breda and painted with camouflage patterns. Captain Tork sat under the shelter, next to a small, carefully contained fire. There were two other people with her.

"This is Sergeant Danna Boran," the doctor said, gesturing to the nearest of them. He was clearly Pack, his face that of a dark furred wolf, with yellow eyes that watched Clifford with unflinching intensity. He wore a ragged grey poncho over camo-pattern body armour. A long-barrelled gun lay across his lap, one finger tapping close to the trigger. He gave Clifford a slow, silent nod.

"And this is Private Axio Marel."

The third soldier looked up from the pot he'd been stirring. He'd set aside the upper half of his body armour, to reveal bulging muscles under a tight t-shirt with the Valtech Corporation's diamond logo. He was young looking, his sun-browned skin as smooth as Clifford's, except for the blond stubble across his scalp and jaw. He wore some kind of electronic comms bracer around his left wrist, with a skull sticker on the strap.

"Folks, this is Clifford Foster. He arrived today."

"Great to meet you, mate," Marel said. "Pull up a seat. We caught a bird; I'm stewing it up with ration bars and that."

"Please tell me you checked it for infection before you got close." The doctor took the seat next to Marel, and Clifford the one next to her.

"Course we did. No veins, no pale bits, nothing. We listen, don't we, sarge?"

Boran nodded and watched them across the pot, his gaze as hard as any weapon. Clifford had to fight the instinct to run away and hide.

"Remember, don't approach anything—"

"White or dusty or that moves funny." Marel tapped his spoon against the side of the pot, then against the side of his head. "We remember, Doc, don't you worry."

"Yet you still need treatment." Solvesdin opened her bag. "What did you do this time?"

"There was this bush." Marel held his right arm out toward her, revealing a red rash that grew fainter the further it got from his wrist. "It had these weird red fruits, right, and you said fruit and veg was safe."

"From the chalk rot, yes, but plants can be dangerous in

their own way."

"I know that now. It burst when I touched it, and this stinging shit ran down my sleeve, burning like a volcano."

"Acid?" Captain Tork asked.

"Given what else I've seen, more likely an alkali." The doctor pressed a sensor against the reddened skin and Marel's jaw tightened. "Have you got anything to drink? I'm parched."

The captain poured water from a plastic can into cups and passed them around. Both the cannister and the cups had Valtech diamonds moulded into them. Clifford was about to take a sip, but Doctor Solvesdin stopped him.

"You'll want one of these," she said, pulling a straw from a pocket and putting it in her cup. "Filters out the bacteria. I've got more in the cab."

"Here." The captain tossed one across the fire. Clifford fumbled the catch, but at least it landed in his lap.

"Careful, these folks will charge rent on that," Solvesdin said. Boran and Marel laughed.

"That's the way the world works, Doc," Marel said. "Most of us don't live in your hippy communes."

"Your rules don't apply down here," she said, spreading a salve across his arm.

"Not my rules, just the market, innit Cap?"

Tork pointed at the straw in Clifford's hand. "Consider it an investment."

Clifford had met corporate types before. One of his friends from school, Stibb, had even signed up with Valtech, a different route off the farm from the one Clifford had taken. But he'd never spent much time around them, didn't know how seriously to take any of this.

"It's not much of an investment," he said, turning the thick straw between his fingers, noting the diamond logo on the filter section. "I mean, I'll be dead soon, right?"

"I told you already," Solvesdin said. "It ain't over. What more proof do you need than this?"

Clifford looked around the shelter. No one was coughing or feverish with infection. None of their skin was swollen or marred by thick, dark veins. The worst injury any of them had was a rash. There was shelter, medicine, food cooking over a fire, and outside the shelter, the rain was fading away.

Tork's wrist beeped, and she looked down at a bracer like Marel's.

"Time to eat," she said. "Then sleep. We need to be ready for the crystals."

Clifford raised his hand, curious about what these crystals were. But instead of calling on him to speak, Tork pointed at a bowl Boran was holding out.

"Later."

Clifford tasted a spoonful of the food. Salt, sugar, and additives bludgeoned his tongue, but his mouth started watering, and his stomach rumbled a demand. Clifford grinned as he spooned the stew into his mouth.

Maybe he really would live.

Chapter Three

Clifford stared in mute awe at the fungus emerging between the roots of the vast trees. Its grey flesh grew before his eyes, centimetres emerging each minute, an impossible speed.

Seeing the crystals had been amazing enough. Waking at dawn beneath the Valtech team's shelter, his eyes had been drawn to those angular purple shapes scattered across the ground outside. He'd never seen anything like it, not on farms or fieldwork or in any of his textbooks, finger-long crystals expressing out of the earth in the aftermath of rain. The crystals changed the whole world around them, scattering the sunlight in beautiful blue fragments.

That light could have emerged from a tall tale of the Ossian terraformers, a world remade in strange and fascinating forms. Legends said that half the inhabited planets in the galaxy had been reshaped by the Ossians, those elusive engineers rebuilding entire biosystems before moving on to their next challenge. But the myths about Abaddon painted it as a hellscape, not a miracle of ingenious reinvention.

While Clifford knew some inorganic chemistry, it wasn't enough to understand the ways the crystals shouldn't be happening. Fungus, on the other hand, he understood. It was a vital part of the soil cycle, the fruit above ground representing only a fraction of the wonders below, and this fraction was growing faster than any he had ever seen.

"Amazing, ain't it?" Doctor Solvesdin said. Like Clifford, she'd put on plastic glasses to protect her eyes and a filter mask over her mouth and nose, but he could hear the smile in her voice. "A miracle where only we'll see it."

"I'm sure there's a rational explanation. A complex mycelial network, supported by specific soil chemistry. I wonder what other organisms it lives in sympathy with. I should get my sampling kit and—"

"Save that for later. Right now, we need to gather them. It's a long time since the last big storm, and everyone's running low."

Around them, others were roaming the forest floor: Captain Tork and Private Marel; a wild-haired man called Farringer in a tattered flight suit; three people in furs who seemed to be together but never spoke, just glanced around with wide, nervous eyes. The doctor wasn't the only one who'd driven into the heart of the storm to see what it left.

Clifford snapped the fungus off its stalk and put it in a sack made from the plastic cloth of an old tent. He fought the temptation to stay and watch whether the fungal stump grew back, but moved on across the rich ground to pluck the next one. Solvesdin stayed nearby, working so much faster that she could already have moved on. From all he'd been told, that would have been the rational thing to do, gathering precious resources while she had a chance. He appreciated the effort she made to teach him, all the more so because it cost her.

The others worked their way quickly across the ground, filling boxes and sacks. They'd done the same with the crystals that morning, then rested until the fungus emerged. The conversation was stuttering, uncertain, ragged scraps of human connection that were still better than nothing. The group in furs worked in focused silence, responding with uncertain smiles to Marel's brash banter.

The only one who didn't collect was Sergeant Boran. He had disappeared up a tree at the start of the day, clawed fingers digging into the bark, his rifle slung across his shoulder and a set of binoculars clipped to his belt. Clifford had quickly lost sight of him, but he was up there somewhere, watching over them.

"I had no idea there were people living down here," Clifford said as Solvesdin led him to the next rich patch of fungal growth.

"How would you? Nobody leaves, remember. Too much risk of infection."

"So, we're stuck here for the rest of our lives." His shoulders slumped. Without proper shelter, hospitals, or agriculture, stuck on a planet with chalk rot and the swarm, the rest of his life wouldn't last long.

"As the Book of Spring says, 'His holy wind carries us where we are needed, that the seeds of His holy will may grow.'"

She laid a hand on Clifford's shoulder, an intrusion that he fought not to shrug off.

"I don't believe in those things," he said. "Not God or your wind, not miracles or fate. Just what the evidence shows."

"That's cool." She returned to her picking. "God doesn't need everyone to believe, just enough to keep the universe alive."

"You really believe that?"

"Uh-huh."

She took off her knitted cap. A beam of bright sunlight pierced the canopy, illuminating her, and something thicker than sweat seeped across her bare scalp.

"Shaving your head, is that a sign of your faith?" he asked. Solvesdin laughed.

"No, child. The chlorophyll skin, the adapted teeth, the magneto-receptors, even this..." She ran a finger across her scalp and held it out so that he could see the mucus. "Those choices let me settle where God needs His seeds to grow. But the hair? That's all about me."

A shrill whistle pierced the air. Farringer jolted upright, his tattered flight suit stretching as he twisted left and right, staring fearfully around. Then he grabbed his sack and scurried away.

"Boran's spotted movement," Solvesdin said. "Most fauna here avoid the unfamiliar, so if it's coming this way, it's swarm."

"Should we leave?" Clifford clutched his sack tight in a sweaty hand. Across the clearing, the trio in furs kept working, though they moved faster than before.

"Not yet. That boy's got good eyes, he can sense trouble from miles away, and we need to wait for the rats."

"Rats?"

"Technically, they're not even mammals, but you'll know them when you see them."

She handed him a fresh sack, reinforced with supple wires, and a pair of thick gloves.

"Get them alive if you can. It affects the hormonal content of their blood, which affects the longevity of the serum."

"It's made with rat blood?" This felt like the first week on the station, when the bored crew had spent hours hazing him. The part of him that learned the hard way about polka dot paint frowned in disbelief at a medicine of rats' blood, mushrooms, and crystals.

"I get your cynicism, but I've been here five years, and it takes lifetimes for scientists to make sense of an ecosystem, so I can't give you the answers you need. Just take the gloves and do the job, while I stow these on Breda."

Carrying their sacks of fungi, she headed back to the truck.

Private Marel was standing by a hole among the roots, also wearing thick gloves. A box with spiked wire around its open top stood nearby. He looked up as Clifford approached.

"What's up, Cliff?"

"It's Clifford."

"Whatever."

"Are we really meant to catch rats?"

"Why d'you think I'm standing over this bloody hole?" Marel frowned as his bracer beeped. "Keep an eye on this one for a minute: a big hole means a whole family, and I don't want them getting away."

Clifford stood over the hole, adjusting his mask, while Marel started running on the spot.

"Got to get enough exercise in every morning," the soldier explained, waving his bracer. "Otherwise, my health insurance goes up."

"You're stranded on a plague planet and you're worried about health insurance costs?"

"Aren't you?" Marel dropped to the ground and started doing push-ups. "I keep my premiums down this quarter, I can buy the VL206, which means I'm equipped for grade four missions. Grade four means proper bonuses." Still pushing himself up and down on one arm, he tapped the side of his head. "You've always got to plan ahead, always got to be in action. That's what makes a winner."

The bracer bleeped.

"That's better." Marel got back to his feet and came to stand by the hole. "Now let's get some rats."

As if in response, a snuffling sound emerged. Marel pressed a finger to his lips.

A creature waddled out. It was the size of a large rodent, covered in spines so slender they were almost fur, with three pairs of beady black eyes positioned around its stubby head. A ring of whiskers twitched as it emerged into the air, a bare tail swishing behind.

Six more creatures followed the first. After Marel's comment about families, Clifford expected some of them to be smaller, but they were all around the same size. The first and last out had darker spines than the rest.

Marel held up a hand, then counted down on his fingers. When he got to one, the two of them dived in, each grabbing one of the creatures. The captured rats squealed, and the others started running.

"Into the box!" Marel said. "We'll split them later."

Clifford dumped his first rat into Marel's box then ran after another. The creatures had short legs and broad paws, and he had no trouble catching up with their waddling run. He grabbed one, its spines pressing against the thick cloth of the gloves, and ran with it back to the box.

"Runner!" Marel shouted, pointing at a pale creature about to disappear between the roots.

Clifford grabbed the creature's tail as it dived for another hole. There was a moment's resistance, then the creature popped out in a spray of dirt, its forepaws flapping. Clifford carried it in triumph to the box. His heart was racing, but for the first time since he'd crashed on Abaddon, it wasn't with fear.

"Three for you, four for me," Marel said, assessing their catch. "Not bad, but we can do better."

He pointed to a clump of fungus where a pale rodent was chewing on the soft grey flesh.

"There'll be more with that one. Come on."

Within an hour, the box was full of squirming bodies, contained by electrified wire around the top. Clifford and Private Marel sat down to divide their winnings.

"What brought your team here?" Clifford asked as he held his sack open.

"Just another job." Marel picked up a rat. "High risk, high pay, huge bonus if we succeed. Figured I'd take a chance."

He dropped the rat into Clifford's sack and reached for another. Across the clearing, Farringer and a man in furs were getting in each other's way as they both tried to grab the same rat.

"You chose to be down here?" Clifford stared in bewilderment at Marel.

"Like I said, high risk job, but high reward."

"What sort of job?"

"What do you think?" Marel laughed as he flung another rat in. Like the first one, it was on the small side, with pale spines. "No corporation's ever going to admit to breaking the blockade, any more than they'd let someone else fly out. But the first group to get working samples of this place, to analyse it, to monetise a cure for the chalk rot..." He tapped his bracer. "That's the big bucks, that is."

"For them, maybe, but you'll be stuck down here, waiting for the swarm to get you."

"Management gave Captain Tork an extraction plan. Once we get something R and D can monetise, she triggers the plan and whoosh, we're out."

"What sort of plan?"

Marel shrugged. "That's above my pay grade, innit?"

"Seems like a big risk."

Clifford peeled off his gloves and spread sanitiser from a tube across his hands. He didn't want to risk picking up something off the rats; chalk rot was more than enough to be worrying about.

A whistle sounded from above, two bursts this time. Marel started working faster.

"You've got to grind, Cliff, or you'll spend your whole life in some dead end job. Me, I've got a vision. Twenty good years as a merc, invest my earnings, live off them. And when I say live, I mean really live. Penthouse apartment. Latest fashions. New car every year. Drinking flash cocktails in strip clubs. I'm gonna live like a millionaire, mate, and to do that, I've got to take the big jobs."

Clifford was glad that his mask hid his expression. This was a child's idea of what a good life meant, one lived on animal instinct, yet Marel seemed perfectly sincere, enthusiastic even.

"I wish you luck," Clifford said, and bowed his head as respectfully as he could.

"Thanks, mate. What about you, what do you want out of life?"

"My own research cohort. Good publications and the respect of my peers." And the nice house of course, spouse and children, but those weren't things one said out loud.

"Good for you." Marel picked a lump of something off the ground, turned it over in his hands, tossed it away. "Let's get this haul back to the transports."

Carrying his squirming sack, Clifford followed Marel. The soldier walked with a confidence that he could only envy, sure in his footing and in his future. The whole Valtech team seemed like this: fit, healthy, adaptable, good people to work with if he wanted to survive.

And he did want to survive, to get that research team, those publications, the house and the family. The aching oblivion he'd felt after the crash was still in his mind, threatening to surge up and swallow him, but if there was a sliver of hope then he could hold it back. Hope to live, a little longer at least. Hope for more, perhaps, though he couldn't allow himself that yet. The higher he dreamed, the further he could fall.

There was a warbling whistle, then the crack of a shot.

"Shit!" Marel picked up speed, running as best he could with the box. Clifford ran after him, branches whipping his face as he shoved his way through the undergrowth, his breath coming hard through his mask. The sack of rats bounced against his back, their awkward weight slowing him.

Another shot, and another.

"Report!" Captain Tork's voice burst out of Marel's bracer.

"Swarm at fifty." Sergeant Boran's voice this time, then another shot. "Came along dead ground, hidden by leaves. Some now at forty."

A shot again.

"Evac!" Tork shouted, her voice echoing through the trees for everyone to hear.

Clifford burst through the foliage into the clearing where they'd parked the trucks. Marel was halfway to Valtech's sleek transport. Breda lay beyond that, doors open, Doctor Solvesdin waving at Clifford.

"Forget the rats!" she yelled.

But he couldn't forget the rats. The rats meant medicine. The rats meant life. In some mad way, the rats were his hope of survival.

Boran dropped from the branches onto the roof of the Valtech transport. He landed in a crouch, levelled his rifle, fired. As Marel climbed in, the transport's engine started.

Halfway across the clearing, Clifford saw swarm emerging. They were big ones, lurching along on two legs, four, six, swollen bodies swaying as they picked up speed.

His heart hammered as he ran, the sack squirming against his back, rats screeching for release. The glasses fell off his nose and crunched underfoot.

The camouflaged transport moved. Boran was still on the roof, steadying himself as they accelerated.

The swarm reached the people in furs before they could start their truck. One of them disappeared under a bear with patchy fur and a swollen eye. Another went down fighting, swinging a shovel but unable to resist the crush.

One of the swarm was ahead of the rest, closer to Breda than Clifford. It was a human body, half naked, dark veins pulsing, eyes bulging. Blood from a fallen scavenger spattered its bone white skin. Seeing a human succumbed to the rot made Clifford want to scream, but all his breath was taken with running.

The doctor had started the engine, but she couldn't see the creature coming. Dread swept like darkness through Clifford.

A shot. The swarm thing fell. Clifford jumped over its body, slung the sack into Breda, scrambled in and slammed the door shut. A body rammed into the back of the truck, but they were moving, accelerating faster than the swarm, leaving death behind.

Clifford stared at the wing mirror, watching what they'd left. The furred people's truck rocked and the last of them fell out the door. The swarm fell on him.

Clifford turned away, pushing the void back down. Ahead, Sergeant Boran sat strapped to the roof of the transport, his rifle in his hands. Clifford looked from him to Doctor Solvesdin, her green lips whispering a prayer, the woman who had said they shouldn't bring guns.

Had he joined the wrong team?

Chapter Four

Clifford held the vibrating grinder in place on the folding table, careful not to obscure its solar charger. The grinder was a kitchen implement Solvesdin had retrieved from a downed shuttle, while the charger came from an old set of solar lanterns. The wires connecting them together weren't neat, but they worked.

After a count of twenty, he released the button that engaged the motor, took the lid off, tipped the purple dust into an old coffee can, and refilled the grinder with crystals before starting again. He pushed a face shield made from a clear plastic bottle up his face, protection against dust in his eyes. This was the simplest part of the process, and the least interesting, but that was to be expected. He had to prove himself one step at a time.

The first batch of medicine was already brewing. Doctor Solvesdin had set up her still next to Breda, explaining each part and its function as she went along. Clifford was due to help her disassemble it at the end, to reinforce that learning.

While the device bubbled and steamed, the doctor butchered and bled the rats, a process made no more pleasant by the way that she looked each one in the eye and apologised before slitting it open. Clifford had considered asking if she had earplugs to shut out the squealing, but blocking his senses seemed like a bad idea when the swarm were out there, hungry beasts hunting uninfected flesh. Even the smells of blood and mineral dust were helping keep him alert.

They'd set up camp on top of a bare hill between a river and the forest. The Valtech team were with them again, as was Farringer, the wild-haired man in the tattered flight suit with whom they'd gathered ingredients. Apparently, he was some sort of officer from the Earldom of Esten, yet he never gave anyone their titles and he hadn't washed his hands once. Clifford was shocked to see a man of rank fallen so far.

The parts of the still were relatively simple, and each group had improvised one using their own equipment and components salvaged from crash sites. The Valtech team's was the newest, its parts not yet stained and crusted, but also the least reliable. Every so often, steam would burst from one of its joints and Private Marel would start cursing while Captain Tork silently reconnected the pipes.

"How did you learn to make this?" Clifford asked between the roar of the grinder and the squeals of the rats.

"An older survivor taught me, just after I arrived," Solvesdin said. "Since then, I've tried to reach new arrivals before they got sick, so that I could teach them."

She dropped an exsanguinated rat in a bucket at her feet, then opened the sack to take out a fresh one.

"Who did that survivor learn it from?"

"From someone before her, who learned it from someone before them, on and on back."

"But who worked it out in the first place? And how?"

"Winds know." Solvesdin shrugged. "What matters is that the serum exists."

"Someone had to invent this, despite everything happening here. They had to teach it to people. And those people had to keep passing it down, in the face of the rot and the swarm, and we should be dead, and it doesn't make any sense and..."

Clifford realised that everyone was looking at him. He lowered his trembling hands and tried to take deep breaths. Flashes of the past two days filled his mind. The station. The jungle. The swarm. People whose names he never knew being torn apart.

"It can't last," he said quietly. "We're dead already."

"Stop trying to look for an easy way out."

"Easy?" Clifford stared at Solvesdin. "You think it's easy to accept that I'm doomed?"

"You want us all to accept it, because that saves you from the burden of having to live."

"Well, why not?" His voice rose again, but this time he didn't care. "How long does anyone live here—days, weeks, months? All of them filled with fear, running from monsters and scrabbling in the dirt, gutting rats and grinding rocks. I've almost certainly got the rot already, and all this does—" He pointed at the still. "—is postpone it for a few more hours."

"Life is always a process of dying, a continuum from one state to the other." She took off her hat, ran a hand across her shaved scalp. "Embrace what that gives you."

"That gives me fear." Clifford thumped a fist against his chest, where the void lay. "Fear and pain every waking moment since I reached this awful planet."

"That's why it ain't easy." Solvesdin turned back to address her rat. "I'm sorry for this. May the wind carry you to peace."

Her knife slid up, the rat's squeal fell silent, and its blood ran into her bowl.

Clifford stared at her. This was what mystification did to people, filled their heads with warped philosophies.

But as he turned back to his work, as his heartbeat slowed with the regular rhythm of the task, a sense of shame flashed through him. Solvesdin was a doctor, she was older, she understood this world better than he did. He might not agree with her, but he should learn from her, and he should show respect.

"I'm sorry," he said, bowing his head and turning to face her again. "I..."

Beyond the doctor, a shuttle streaked across the sky, smoke streaming from its engines. It hit the forest, smashing through one of the great trees, and disappeared beneath the canopy. There was an almighty crash, then a thud, and fresh smoke billowed a mile away.

"Come on." Solvesdin set her rats aside and headed for Breda's cab. "There might be survivors."

*

This crash had been more destructive than Clifford's. Coming in at a sharp angle into tall growth, the shuttle hadn't skimmed its way across the ground but ploughed straight in, flinging out earth and broken plants. The remains of the shuttle itself, in the bottom of the crater, were charred, buckled plates and twisted framework, scattered supplies and shattered components. Two broken bodies, all in red, dangled from a gap in what remained of the hull.

Even as Clifford stared, Solvesdin scrambled down the crater, steadying herself with one hand while the other held her medical bag.

"Come on," she said. "There might be survivors."

"There might be supplies," Captain Tork said. "Boran, you're on watch. Marel, with me."

Farringer followed them down, an empty sack over his shoulder.

"You going?" Boran asked, a feral grin spreading across his furred face, exposing a row of sharp white teeth. "Or are you staying up here with me?"

"I'll help," Clifford squeaked, and hurried over the lip, down the broken dirt into the pit.

The place smelled of smoke, churned earth, and fuel. This wasn't a safe place, but where on Abaddon was? Clifford lost his footing, slid the last ten meters, wound up on the ground between Marel and Solvesdin, who were staring into a gap in the wrecked shuttle's hull.

A figure emerged, cartoonishly exaggerated, nearly seven feet tall and bright red, their outline smoothed out by metal plates. The blank face was only broken by the black lenses of visual sensors. A soft whine of miniaturised motors and a hiss of sliding pistons accompanied every move. The armoured space suit of a Red Blade raider.

The raider stopped for a moment, gauntlet resting on the torn plates of the hull, then stepped into the open, feet thudding in the dirt.

"I am Fifth-Blade Dagran," she said, her voice broadcast by speakers in the helmet. "Who are you people?"

"My name's Doctor Emieke Solvesdin." The doctor smiled as she held up her medical bag. "You've had a rough landing. Would you like me to check you for injuries?"

"Stay back." Dagran pointed a pistol that Clifford could barely have carried. "All of you."

Solvesdin raised her hands, and Clifford, still in the dirt, did the same. His heart pounded loudly. No one had ever pointed a gun at him before, and it put a sharp edge back on his blunted terror. Marel raised a pistol of his own, pathetically small in the face of Dagran's weapon. Captain Tork was nowhere to be seen.

"You are exposed," Dagran growled. "Unclean. Infected."

"We're perfectly safe, and if you'll take off your armour then I can—"

Dagran grabbed Solvesdin, hauling her off her feet.

"Give me your supplies and tell me everything you know, then I might leave you to die of the rot."

"I ain't got the rot," Solvesdin croaked. "I have medicine."

"Weak lies. Tell me where I can find a ship."

"No ships. No escape. We—" Solvesdin gagged as Dagran's grip tightened.

Marel fired, three laser blasts square into Dagran's chest. All they left was charred black spots. Solvesdin jerked, throwing off Dagran's aim as the raider fired. Marel dived behind the wreckage, but Farringer fell, blood spraying from his shoulder.

Clifford went skittering across the dirt, desperate for cover. More shots tore into the ground where he had been. He flung himself behind the remains of an engine exhaust, the air shimmering hot above it.

"Throw down your arms and come out," Dagran bellowed, "or I crush this one's throat then come for you."

Clifford crouched in the dirt. His legs were shaking, heartbeat hammering in his ears. He didn't dare look out for fear of being shot, yet he couldn't escape the compulsion to see that terrible red figure, to know the horror coming for him. Almost against his will, he raised his head, peering through the heat haze.

Farringer lay groaning, blood darkening the dirt around him. A few meters away, Marel crouched behind a heap of buckled hull, pistol in his hands. Dagran faced them, Solvesdin swinging from her over-sized fist, twitching and gasping.

Something moved in the gap of the ship's hull. Captain Tork slid silently from the darkness, a broad knife in her hand. With one finger, she tapped a button on her bracer. A light flashed in the same position on Marel's.

At that signal, Marel stood and fired, shots glancing off Dagran's armour. She raised her pistol at him.

Tork lunged. Her knife slashed across the back of Dagran's neck, slicing through a joint in the suit. Something hissed. Dagran jerked. Solvesdin fell from her grasp. Tork grabbed Dagran's head, twisted, wrenched the helmet off and flung it aside.

At last, Clifford saw Dagran's face. It seemed absurdly small against the bulk of her armoured body.

"You shit!" She wheeled around, swinging her pistol.

With the crack of a gunshot, Dagran's head exploded. Blood streamed out, red on red, but her body stayed upright, frozen by the armour.

Clifford puked. The liquid hissed as it hit the hot wreckage, and the acrid steam forced him to step away. He stumbled and fell staring at the horror show.

"Good work, Boran," Tork called out. "You stay in place. Marel, with me, we're checking for more."

As matter of fact as any bureaucrat, Tork walked away.

*

It was the strangest burial Clifford had ever seen. Tork planted explosives around the edge of the crater, then triggered them once they'd finished scavenging for supplies. Dagran, her raider crew and their ship's wreckage disappeared beneath violently dislodged dirt.

As dusk fell, Clifford and Marel sat on the roof of the Valtech transport, watching the dust and smoke settle. Marel had Dagran's pistol in his lap and occasionally lifted it in an experimental sort of way, the muscles in his arm bulging at the strain. Solvesdin was sitting on a folding chair outside Breda, hooked up to an intravenous drip and eating insects from a tin. A few feet from her, snoring rumbled from the Iyer Systems ground car where Farringer slept off sedatives and surgery. Tork sat on a rock polishing her boots, while somewhere in the shadows Boran lurked, always watching.

With meticulous care, Clifford rubbed at the cracks of his knuckles with a soft, damp cloth. He'd been doing the same thing for the past hour, but nothing seemed to get out the last traces of dirt, the places where disease festered.

"What do you think they were doing here?" Clifford asked. The steady work on his hands had finally stopped him shaking but he still felt numb, the edges of his mind as distant as those of his body. "The Red Blade, I mean?"

"Robbing one of the stations," Marel said. "Or trying to get rot samples for a bioweapon. You know what those wankers are like."

Clifford only knew the pirates by reputation, monsters in horror stories and lurid news from the shipping lanes, but he nodded as if he understood.

"It's strange, isn't it?" he said. "First my station malfunctions, then Dagran's people get shot down. So much destruction in a few days."

"Didn't they tell you anything about this place?" Marel polished the pistol with a soft cloth. "It's a full-blown CZ, just no one admits it."

"CZ?"

"Combat zone." Marel held up the pistol. "Blades out, safeties off, every wanker for himself."

"But this is the quarantine zone, our blockade is all that stands between humanity and the chalk rot. It's the one place in the universe where everyone cooperates."

"Yeah, right." Marel laughed. "They sent you here to nick soil samples, us to grab what we could, those red tossers to do who knows what. You call that cooperation?"

"I saw the stations when I came in, the warships too..."

"Warships. Exactly. They're in orbit for the same reason so many people are down here. This planet's unique, innit. Everybody wants a piece, and nobody dares let the others have one. So, there they are, constantly trying to sneak something past each other, and slapping down anyone who comes close. None of them can admit it in public, because they've got to keep up the quarantine." He tapped his bracer. "Told you, this is why it's worth the big bucks."

Clifford pressed his hands against his temples. There was a madness to this place.

"Tell you what, Cliff, you help us find something useful, maybe we'll take you out with us. How does that sound?"

It sounded like a life restored, and it sounded impossible, the sort of hollow promise that made the void gape wide.

"You know about dirt and that, right?" Marel continued, cloth sliding across the pistol's barrel. "Maybe you can work out how those crystals and mushrooms come up, turn the serum into a proper cure. Monetise that and we're set for life."

"It's not that easy." Clifford shook his head. There were so many gaps in Marel's get rich plan. "We don't even know how the serum holds off the rot."

"So, work it out."

"I'm a soil scientist, not a medic."

"But it's all about that soil, innit?"

Clifford sighed. He could have said many things about Marel, but the man knew how to dream big. Right now, Clifford didn't dare dream past tomorrow.

"Shouldn't you be making the Captain's dinner?" he asked, looking for a distraction.

"Why would I do that?"

"Because she's your Captain."

"I'm a soldier, not a fucking servant."

"She's your superior. It would be beneath her dignity to cook for herself when you're here."

"Fuck her dignity. I worked hard to get where I am, I'm not gonna start polishing some tosser's boots." Marel held up the pistol. "See this? This is what happens when you put the work in."

"But you didn't—"

"Fuck off back to the Doc's truck, go cook up some dignity for her."

Chapter Five

It was quiet as death by the river, the waters sliding past solemn and silent, an expanse so wide that the far bank became a line, a border penned between the waters and the towering trees. Something flew beyond those trees, a shape that Clifford might have mistaken for a distant shuttle, if he hadn't known where he was. More likely a bird and a trick of perspective, or some illusion created by air currents. Every atmosphere had some visual glitch, whether it was auroras at the poles, condensates over hidden volcanoes, or the lightning webs that appeared on winter nights back home. The mind looked for patterns to make sense of the world, and nature obliged.

Clifford hunched over his folding table, shifting samples of soil from one container to another, adding them to solutions, placing careful drops in the open mouths of measuring devices. These past few weeks were the most use his testing kit had ever had. Every night, when he took out the photo of his parents and offered them thanks for his life, he offered Aunt Prein his gratitude too.

The remains of concrete foundations protruded from the mud of the nearby riverbank, carved stone blocks further down. Strange to think that this planet had once supported settled, stable colonies, not just desperate people fleeing the swarm. How far back had that been? He wished he'd paid attention to that part of the briefing, but it hadn't caught his attention in the same way as the science. He didn't even know how much history was recorded for this place, how much was lost to the flow of time.

A sound made him sit bolt upright, attentive for what came next until familiar footfalls emerged.

"I'm around here, Doctor Solvesdin," he called out.

She appeared around the end of Breda, a sack in one hand and a basket in the other. He'd watched her weave that basket in the evenings, sitting secure in the back of the truck, hooked up to her mysterious IV drip.

"Learned anything yet, Clifford?" she asked. From one of his superiors back at the university, that would have been a challenge, the real question being why he hadn't learned more. The first few times she'd asked, he'd tightened up, a defence at the ready, but slowly he was learning to accept encouragement for what it was.

"Actually, I have." He pointed to a readout on one of the devices, a coppery box with a hole in the top and screens to either side. "Remember about the cation exchange capacity?"

"Uh-huh." She settled into the seat he'd put out next to his own, a padded seat salvaged from his own shuttle. "It measures how nutritious the soil is."

"Near enough. And you remember I commented on how extraordinary it is here?"

"But the life in the soil ain't accessing all that nutrition." She took off her hat and then her sweater, revealing a sleeveless shirt and green arms. "You wanted to know why."

"And I think I know." Clifford tapped a purple crystal against the desk. "There's a chemical that's blocking it. Bacteria, nematodes, fungi, all of them, their systems slow down the higher its dosage is."

"Uh-huh." She turned in the seat, orienting her body toward the sun. "Go on. I'm listening."

"So, when the rain falls, that chemical crystallises out. I don't know how or why—"

"A recurring theme on this planet."

"Right, but never mind that now." Crystals rattled as Clifford's jiggling knee bounced off the underside of the table. "What matters is that the blocking chemical leaves the soil, forming those crystals we collect. In its absence, all that richness is suddenly available. Some of the fungus is straining so hard against the blocker that, once the nutrients are accessible, it shoots up, leading to those mushrooms."

"Uh-huh." Solvesdin sat a little straighter, looking from Clifford to the crystals and back again. "I guess that makes sense."

"More than that, though. If the blocker obstructs growth in organisms arising in this ecosystem, then maybe that's why it's important to the serum, because it can hold back the chalk rot."

"That's fantastic!" For a moment, excitement lit up her face, but then she grimaced and sat back. "No, it's too neat. I want to believe it, but for the pattern to be able to replicate inside a human body? It doesn't make sense for a system to evolve that way."

"Oh." Clifford looked away and his voice fell. "I thought you believed in miracles."

"I do, but I know medicine, and this ain't the way God works."

"Then maybe somebody else did it." Clifford kicked at the dirt beneath the desk.

"Let's not go looking for the devil." She laid a hand on his shoulder. None of his previous superiors would have made such a gesture. "You've achieved something amazing here, Clifford, discovered something no one else understood. A lot's still missing, and that's cool, we'll find it later. As the Book of Summer says, 'Relish my light while it lasts, and winter's cold when it comes.'"

"I'll try."

"That's my guy." She stood up. "I'll cook us dinner. I found some rabbit-like creatures with no sign of infection, a nest of nice fat grubs, and more of those purple tubers."

"I should do the cooking."

"That's mighty kind, but it's my turn."

He smiled. "Thank you, Doctor Solvesdin."

"No problem."

She headed into the back of Breda and pans clattered about. Then her head poked out of an open hatch.

"Did I tell you I spotted the Valtech folks, around the river bend? Figure they've spotted the new storm forming, same as us. How about we face it together?"

"That sounds good." Much as he respected Solvesdin, he wanted to see other people, to have something like society again. "Thank you."

"No problem, Clifford."

"Um..." He looked away, caught on a thought he couldn't quite express.

"Yes?"

He looked up at her. "If you want, you could call me Cliff."

She beamed. "If you finally call me Emi."

*

Over a dozen people sat around a campfire, the largest gathering of Abaddon's nomad survivors that Clifford had seen so far. He'd met some of them in passing, but not enough to have a handle on their status. Emi Solvesdin's informal greetings were no help, and a day of gathering ingredients in the rain-soaked forest hadn't let him assess the hierarchy. To avoid embarrassing himself, he kept to his side of the fire, among the familiar figures of the Valtech team, enjoying the smell of wood smoke and listening to the others talk.

"You know what I miss?" Private Marel asked.

"No, but you're going to tell us," Sergeant Boran said, rolling his yellow eyes. Clifford, sitting between them on a log, laughed nervously, not wanting to offend a man who could tear his throat out with his teeth.

"I miss protein shakes. I mean, these are all right..." Marel held up a supplement pill. "But I've got to eat a meal with it, and that takes time. When you've got shakes, you can gulp it down in two minutes, set you up for half the day."

He popped the pill in his mouth and washed it down with water from his Valtech branded cup. Unlike the others, his cup had red enamel in the diamond logo.

"I thought you wanted the finer things in life," Clifford said.

"This ain't the finer things." Marel held up a half-eaten tuber, its outer layer blackened from roasting in the fire. "Besides, I've got to be efficient while I'm still working, get the most out of every minute. That's how you earn those big bucks."

He tapped his bracer right by the skull sticker. Boran made

a mocking imitation of the gesture on his off wrist, and a bracelet of fangs rattled. Marel stuck his middle finger up at his colleague and the two of them sniggered.

Clifford tried to hold his expression steady as a secret thrill ran through him. He would never have dared to talk or act like this, especially the way Marel did, swearing at a superior. He ought to be appalled, but then he imagined doing it to his old tutor and caught himself giggling out loud.

"What's got into you, pup?" Boran asked, looking down his snout at Clifford.

"Too much of this, perhaps." Rothsten, an engineer off a Clan Abra blockade station, handed a bottle to Boran, who took a swig, then handed it to Clifford. It was the third time that the liquor, which Rothsten distilled between batches of serum, had made its way around the fire, and Clifford had given up on saying no. It still tasted awful, like hand sanitiser mixed with leaves, but he had to admit, the warmth in his gut was welcome on a cold evening.

As the conversation continued and the bottle passed from hand to hand, Clifford sat back, enjoying the moment. It was strange to think that he was content, but hard to deny. With the stars out, one of the moons high, and firelight brightening the bronze trunks of the nearest trees, the scene was reminiscent of the harvest festival back home. Every family off the local farms and all the labourers from the villages would gather at the station to watch the biggest wagons roll out, then head up to a dell beyond the Stibb Farm. They'd eat and drink, sing songs and dance around a bonfire. He'd kissed a girl for the first time there, and drunk more than he should have at least once, back before he'd learned proper behaviour at college.

He'd never thought that he missed it, but now he found himself calculating how many harvests since he'd been away, wondering if he couldn't have made it back just once.

Too late for that now.

Clifford's gaze fell from the treetops toward the fire. Across from him, face distorted by the flames between them, Captain Tork sat eating quietly between Emi Solvesdin and Farringer, whose arm was still in an inflated support sling. The captain met Clifford's gaze and held it, expressionless, until Clifford looked away.

"...not just the VL206, I'm going to get goggles like the cap's too, whatever brand that is." Marel was talking louder, hands waving in enthusiasm. "The shops back home won't know what hit them when my bonus comes in."

It was nonsense. The whole universe relied on the blockade, and the fates of a few ragged survivors couldn't be allowed to threaten that. None of them were leaving this place, but Marel talked like he believed and that was comforting.

"If you want to play the big dog, go mark some trees," Boran said, his claw flicking a dismissive gesture.

"You know what? I will."

Marel wobbled a little as he stepped over the log and headed into the undergrowth.

"Lightweight." Boran shook his head.

Clifford nodded and looked down, staring at his feet instead of Boran's fur, desperately trying to think of something to say that wasn't about his claws or the gleam in his eyes as his long tongue tasted the air. He doubted that the sergeant would want to hear about the clay content of the local dirt.

"For fuck's sake, get on with it," Boran snapped.

"What?" Clifford flinched.

"You can always tell when someone's not met pack, and they always have some stupid question, so get it out of your system, pup, before you choke on it."

Clifford ought to be offended at the assumption, except that Boran was right. He wanted to ask, but would it still be rude, even after receiving permission?

"I'm giving you one chance, because I'm feeling generous." The soldier held up a clawed finger. "Don't waste it."

Clifford dredged courage from somewhere inside.

"Why a wolf?"

"Because that's what I dreamed, at my coming of age." Boran gazed into the fire and his tone turned wistful. "Running with the pack, strong and agile, my senses alive to the world. I knew it would be a challenge, but I accepted the surgery, mastered the beast within, and came out stronger."

"What if you'd dreamed of a salmon or a pigeon or, I don't know, an ant?"

"I fucking didn't, alright?" Boran glared at him, voice as sharp as his teeth. "I dreamed a fierce beast, and I mastered it."

"Is mastery the best way to relate to nature?" Solvesdin asked across the fire. "Surely our life here, in symbiosis with the storms and their fruit, is proof that humans thrive when we collaborate with God's creation, not wrestle it into submission."

"Weak talk." Boran spat into the flames. "Like I'd expect from a gomish."

The doctor's smile froze. Around the fire, everyone fell silent. Clifford's fingers dug into the wood of his tree trunk seat. Gomish was an Aunt Prein word.

"Sergeant Boran," Tork said quietly. "Doctor Solvesdin is a colleague."

"She's a fucking cultist."

"She's a valuable colleague."

Boran's jaw clenched. Slow breaths swayed his whiskers. Clifford had seen him kill a woman with a single shot, but he'd never seen him look more dangerous.

"My apologies, Doctor Solvesdin." Boran's voice was as stiff as his back. "I should not have said what I did."

"I'm sorry too," Solvesdin said. "I raised a sensitive subject in a clumsy way. I should have considered what it means to you."

She stood up and stepped around the fire, hand outstretched.

Boran's gaze flitted to Tork. There was no change in the captain's expression, but Boran must have read something there because he got to his feet.

Before they could shake, Marel crashed through the undergrowth.

"Look what I caught!" Firelight lit his grin. "People pay a fortune for novelty pets."

He held out his hands. A small, furred face protruded between them, twitching as it sniffed the air.

"What is that?" Solvesdin asked, her compassion for Boran replaced by forced calm.

"It's a bat," Marel said. "But with four wings. That's weird, innit?"

"Are you bleeding?"

"Huh?" Marel looked at the blood running from the back of his hand. "Oh, yeah, the little shit scratched me as I was catching him, even bit a chunk out of my thumb, but it'll be worth it when I mone—"

"Everyone back."

Clifford responded instantly to Solvesdin's tone, leaping away from Marel.

"It's only a bat, innit? Not infected, I checked before I grabbed it." Marel's confidence faded as he spotted Tork standing beside the doctor, pistol in hand. "Cap, what's going on?"

"Doctor?" Tork asked.

"Bats have mighty powerful immune systems," Solvesdin said. "They can fly past almost any barrier, pick up diseases off half a continent, and never show any symptoms. This creature could be a vector for chalk rot."

Most people were backing away from Marel toward the far side of the fire, but Boran and the brewer Rothsten had picked up fallen branches and were circling in, watching Marel's hands.

Marel was looking at his hands too, eyes wide, lip trembling.

"That ain't right," he said, staring at the pale patch around the wound on the back of his hand, white beneath the red of blood, the first dark veins spreading like roots ahead of it. "I took the supplements. I did the exercises. I worked the grind." He looked at Tork. "Cap, this ain't fair."

Marel's hands shifted.

"No, don't!" Clifford shouted, realising a moment too late what was going to happen.

Marel let go of the bat.

As the creature took off, Boran and Rothsten swung their improvised clubs. Boran hit a wing, sending the bat off balance, and it flew into Rothsten's face with a screech, clawing and biting. From across the fire, someone shot a pistol, but the bullet hit Rothsten instead of the bat. He fell against a tree, cursing and weeping, blood streaming from his shoulder.

"Evac!" Tork shouted, and immediately people started to move. Most of them were running. Boran was backing up slowly, the branch in his hand. Clifford drew away from Marel and the fallen Rothsten, away from the stink of blood and the flapping of the bat in the branches above. Only Tork and Solvesdin stood still, the firelight casting its fierce light across blank faces.

"This one's on me," Tork said.

"You don't have to face it alone, Joom," Solvesdin replied. It was the first time Clifford had heard the Captain's forename since their first introduction, and the jarring intimacy of it added to his sense of alarm.

"My people, my mess." Tork raised her pistol. "Go. We'll need you later."

Marel drew a combat knife from his belt and held it to his blood-stained wrist.

"I can cut it off, right?" he asked. "Stop the infection spreading. I can do that, yeah?"

"That's not how it works, Private," Tork said. "We didn't know about the bat, but we both know chalk rot."

Slumped against the tree, Rothsten groaned. The skin was pale around the scratches on his face, dark veins sliding across his cheek.

"But Cap..."

Solvesdin grabbed Clifford's arm.

"We can't leave them," he said, staring at Marel.

"The wind blew you here for a reason, Cliff, and it wasn't to die because some fool picked up a bat."

"But Marel..."

"Sometimes God challenges our empathy and sometimes our capacity to survive, to live on for the sake of others. This is one of those times."

Clifford let her lead him, stumbling and shaking, toward Breda. He could still hear voices, but tried not to hear what they said. Rothsten's groans rose to screams, which were cut short by the sizzle of a laser blast. A second shot followed. After that, the only sounds were the wind in the trees and the nomads' engines disappearing through the woods.

Chapter Six

Beyond the shadow of the frayed awning, scorching sunlight blasted the plains. All around Clifford the dried, yellowing grass curled in upon itself. The soil here was sandy and dry, hardly encouraging for growth. Was the grass dead or just dormant, waiting like the fungus for the rains to come or beaten forever by the extremes of Abaddon's climate?

Clifford asked the same question about himself. Was he dead or just dormant? Marel had thought that he would return from this hell to the real world richer than he'd arrived, but Marel was a body rotting in the woods, his remains consumed by chalk rot and scavengers. Hope was a dangerous thing to have because its broken edges cut so deep.

A movement caught Clifford's eye. He was halfway to his feet before he'd even taken it in, his chair falling to the ground. The dead grass stirred. Was a pale shape moving toward them?

"It's the wind," Solvesdin said. "Like the Book of Summer says, 'His breath whispers over even the most distant star.'"

"What wind? There's no wind."

Then the grass hissed, and the breeze hit him.

"You learn to read this place." Solvesdin smiled up from her reclined shuttle seat, which sat in the sunshine instead of the awning's shade. The brightness of that sunshine had brought out a gleaming coating across her green skin again, a sight that unsettled Clifford more than the IV line from a bag hanging off her chair, the stained end of the tube connecting to a needle in her arm.

"I don't want to learn to read this place. I want to leave." He righted his seat, brushed the dust from its side, and sat down again. "Except that I never will."

He wiped the dust from his hand on a rag, then cleansed both hands with alcoholic gel. It was easier to keep the dispenser out here, next to the equipment on his folding table, than to keep going in and out of Breda, and he didn't trust the local water to keep his hands clean. He imagined the whiteness spreading from the dried cracks in his knuckles like it had emerged with such shocking speed from Marel's scratches, and he reached for the dispenser again.

"How's your analysis going?" Solvesdin asked.

"Intriguing." Clifford tapped one of the test tubes in the rack, in which samples of dirt were floating in different liquids. "Something unexpected is happening in the rhizosphere of the great trees, the area immediately around their roots. The pre-crystalisation pattern works differently, but I'm not sure why."

"Look at you, like some Ossian bio-engineer, reinventing the world we live in."

"I'm not reinventing, just trying to understand."

"Give yourself more credit. Understanding is the first step toward invention."

"I suppose."

He measured soil samples into the next set of tubes, added purified water and a new set of diagnostic chemicals. He was working through his supplies fast, especially since Marel, but what was the point in holding back?

Movement made him jump again, knocking some of the precious chemicals across the table. It was only Solvesdin this time, picking up the half-woven basket that lay next to her chair. Clifford swept the sample back into the tube as best he could, wiped his hands, then cleansed them again.

"Do you want to talk about it?" Solvesdin asked.

He didn't have to ask what "it" she meant. They'd had this conversation every day for a week, Solvesdin talking about the need to process trauma, Clifford determinedly shutting her down. The Brethren could keep their customs if they must, but it was rude to talk about death. Marel was gone and it was appropriate to remember him, but there was no call to dwell on his passing outside of an inquest, and Abaddon had no coroners.

"No thank you, Emi," he said, hoping that the name would placate her.

"What if I want to talk about it?"

"Please, I..." The test tubes shook as he gripped the edge of the table. He remembered the fire distorting their faces, the darkness of the forest, the sickening sizzle of a laser blast.

"You can't hide from death, Cliff."

"I know!" He slammed his palm down on the tabletop. "I know, I know, I know!"

He sank his head into his hands, breath coming in harsh rasps, the scent of sanitiser scouring his senses. Ashamed, he peered out between his fingers, but Solvesdin didn't look shocked or angry. Instead, there was a soft sadness about her expression.

"I don't think you do, Cliff," she said, and tapped the IV bag hanging from her chair. "What do you think this is?"

"I don't know." As long as he didn't ask, he didn't have to face his suspicion.

"Don't you want to know?"

"It's rude to ask about people's health care." He turned his attention back to the table, started sweeping up chemicals to restore them to their tubes. That put dirt and chemicals on his hands, which he forgot to wipe before using the sanitiser, so that the dirt and the alcohol gel formed a grey slick across his fingers, and the fungus was in the dirt and the fungus was death and...

"It's chemotherapy."

He froze. It was rude not to look at someone when they spoke to you, but he couldn't bear to see the IV.

"That's why I'm here," she continued. "I knew that my life was being cut short, so I joined a Brethren expedition to settle Abaddon, to fulfil our mission of bringing God's light to every corner of His creation. Normally that means mountains, deserts, icy wastes, but for a few brave souls, that meant Abaddon. Illegal, of course, and a blockade cruiser shot our engines out on the way in, but that was OK, we weren't planning to leave. After all, God sent us."

"What happened to the others?" Clifford stared down at the dirt on his hands. Asking the question was like picking at a scab, he knew what the results would be, but he couldn't stop himself.

"They all got infected or eaten by swarm in the first few weeks. You really can't build a permanent settlement here."

"And you?"

"The dying woman as survivor? I reckon God likes irony."

Clifford forced himself to look at her, his source of hope transformed into a symbol of despair.

"How long do you have?"

"I don't know, and that's cool with me."

"If you knew, you could plan for the end."

"What would that gain me? I've already lasted longer than I should have done. Maybe it's something to do with this place, or maybe I just got lucky, but either way, He's given me more life than I expected, and I ain't going to waste it worrying about death."

Clifford hung his head. This wasn't how the world was meant to be, and now there was a spatter of dirty goo on the front of his good overalls. He picked up his rag, wiped the stain off, and realised that there was another one further down. He wiped at that too, but it was older, harder to get off, and there was another past that, and a frayed edge, and an area that was starting to fade, and now he wanted to tear off those filthy, stained clothes, but what else was he going to wear?

"I'll leave Breda to you, when the time comes," Solvesdin said, unhooking herself from the IV. "And all my supplies. I can write a will if you want, though I doubt it's needed out here."

"I'm dead without you." Clifford flung the rag down in the dirt. "If Marel can't survive, what chance do I have?"

"Marel?" Solvesdin snorted. "I've seen a dozen corporate expeditions since I've been here, and they never last more than a month."

"They have the kit, the weapons, the fitness. They're so efficient at gathering supplies."

"They work mighty hard." Solvesdin stepped into the shade. "Labouring night and day trying to escape this place, and I've outlasted them all. What does that tell you?"

She headed into the back of Breda, taking her IV bag with her.

Clifford stared at his hands. Just for once, he wanted this place to make sense. The world was meant to reveal itself through study and careful thought, but everything here was backwards: dead creatures walked, bluntness was considered good manners, and his home was the one place that never stayed still. At least when he was studying the soil he didn't face those things.

For the first soil scientist on Abaddon, there were mysteries to be unfurled. One of them was showing itself now, the grey-brown stains on his fingers turning blue like crystals after the rain.

He took one of the precious remaining cotton swabs from his kit, wiped it across the blue, and dropped it into a clean test tube. Then he looked up, and this time the movement in the distance was a white shape, stumbling across the dried grass.

"Time to pack up," Clifford called out. "Swarm are coming in."

*

That night, they parked on a rock plateau raised above the plains. In the centre was a circle where the ground had been flattened and a framework of girders raised, their joints rusted but the metal intact. Old-fashioned and out of place as it was, it took Clifford a few minutes of staring through the windscreen to realise what he was looking at.

"What's a launch platform doing here?" he asked as he handed Solvesdin a bowl of chilli. A cold night was descending beyond Breda's cab, so neither of them wanted to sit outside.

"Launching rockets, I imagine." She wrapped her fingers around the scratched plastic of the bowl. "Or more likely failing to launch them."

"Someone was here long enough to build a rocket?"

"Or brought one down with them. It could be pre-blockade."

Clifford gazed at the skeletal shape, all that remained of people lost to memory.

"Do you think they got out?"

"If they did, then they're still long dead, and so is whatever poor planet or outpost they took the infection to."

When he'd been assigned to the Abaddon study, Clifford had read up on the early chalk rot outbreaks: the infections from station to station, the colonies scoured of human life, the irradiate craters and floating debris from its brutal containment. The origins of the blockade.

He and Solvesdin ate in silence, staring at the launch frame. Those images were why the quarantine mattered, why this place mattered. The need to preserve Abaddon in case it held a cure, and the need to contain it because it definitely held the sickness. Life and death intertwined.

"I'm sorry," he said at last. "About your cancer."

"Thank you." She ate a spoonful of chilli. "I imagine you're feeling sorry for yourself too."

Clifford stared at his bowl. This wasn't about him, but he couldn't help feeling the void gape wider, his own mortality reinforced by the doctor's sickness. Was he supposed to lie to a superior?

"I'm sorry for Marel," he said, turning the bowl in his hands. It was black plastic embossed with Valtech's diamond logo, acquired in a trade of supplies. "All that work he put in, exercising and taking his supplements, doing what his medical tech told him, and it didn't do any good. He didn't get to leave."

"Neither did these folks." Solvesdin pointed her spoon at the launch pad. "Neither does anyone."

Clifford held up his finger, examining its blue stain in the cab's artificial light. He'd spent nearly twenty minutes trying to clean that off, but some stains ran too deep.

"I found something today," he said. "A way of extracting the chemical from the soil without waiting for crystallisation. I think there's a route from this to a synthesised serum."

"Well done, Cliff. So, what's next?"

He wanted to say that it didn't matter, that they were all dead anyway, every moment a futile killing of time. But he couldn't say that to a woman self-administering chemotherapy who'd come to build her people a community and instead helped strangers survive.

There was a difference between lying and not speaking the whole truth.

"Now we tell people," he said. "How can we contact someone off-planet?"

"Signal blocking's part of the blockade, but we can tell other folks on Abaddon. This could make a difference to their lives." From a box under her seat, she took out two syringes of the milky purple serum. "Speaking of which, are you done eating? I want to get us both dosed before we forget."

"I'm done."

Clifford set his black plastic bowl down on the dash and rolled up his sleeve. As he did so, the logo on the bowl caught his eye. Maybe there was another way to use what he knew.

Chapter Seven

Three vehicles roared down the canyon: Breda, the sleek Valtech transport, and Farringer's Iyer Systems ground car. They jolted over dips in the ground and swerved around pillars, while a flame thrower of the roof of Farringer's car spat fire at the swollen, ungainly creatures pursuing them. More swarm were racing along the tops of the canyon walls, flinging themselves off to reach the vehicles, pale and twisted bodies flying against a grey sky.

Clifford gripped his seat tight as one of the swarm, four-legged and with snapping teeth, slammed against the windscreen. Unable to cling on, it slid down, leaving smears across the glass, and Breda lurched as the creature was crushed beneath their wheels.

"Almost clear," Solvesdin said through gritted teeth. She hunched over the controls, sweat seeping from beneath her hat, her face crumpled in concentration. Half a mile ahead, the canyon widened, rock walls falling away.

There was a thud, then movement above their heads. Claws scraped over the roof and a metal plate creaked as it bent. Clifford scrabbled in the foot well for anything he could use as a weapon, but all he found was a tarnished spoon, as futile as it was absurd.

From the roof of the Valtech transport, Boran's rifle barked. The scraping stopped. Something fell. Clifford sagged.

"And we're there." Solvsedin sank in her seat as they emerged from the canyon into a wide river plain. The world opened out before them, mercifully empty of movement, and she accelerated east, chasing the darkest clouds. Soon, they left the swarm behind.

Five miles down the valley, they stopped by the river and Clifford ran out a hose pipe to refill Breda's tanks. His hands didn't shake after every swarm encounter anymore. In fact, he felt almost calm as he stood on the rocks of the riverbank, pipe in hand, watching the other vehicles pull up.

"Hey, Doc," Boran called as he unstrapped himself from the transport's roof. "Can you look at my shoulder? I've strained something."

"I ain't surprised, riding like that." Solvsedin hauled her medical bag out from under her seat. "Are you OK checking over Breda for me, Cliff?"

"I'd be happy to, Emi." He gave her a small, reassuring wave, then returned his attention to the water pipe, watching and listening for blockages. They couldn't afford to have something go wrong with the pump.

Footsteps, slow and steady, approached the river.

"Boran said you wanted to talk." Tork's voice was quiet as the waters whispering by.

Clifford shifted the pipe from one hand to the other, almost dropping it. The water gurgled as he got a firmer grip, keeping the open mouth of the pipe in a still, clear stretch of water.

"Is your extraction still happening?" he asked, keeping his own voice quiet.

"It is."

"When?"

"That's MSI."

"MSI?"

"Mission sensitive information, meaning I won't tell you."

"I have other information that can help with your mission."

Clifford carefully laid the pipe down then pulled a vial from his overalls. It was no larger than the joint of his thumb, a clear plastic container filled with a blue ooze. He handed it to the captain.

"What's this?"

"The chemical that makes up the crystals. I extracted it directly from the soil."

"So?" Tork held the vial up to the light. Her body remained still, her expression tightly controlled.

"The way I did it tells us how the chemical works and could lead to artificial synthesis. We don't have facilities for that here, but out past the quarantine, this has value."

"You want to trade it for extraction."

"Exactly. You were sent here to bring back value—this is your pay day."

Tork handed the vial back to Clifford.

"I have my pay day. All I need is samples of the crystals, the mushrooms, and the rats. Knowing that there's a serum to fend off the rot, that's a success for our stakeholders."

Clifford's shoulders drooped. He looked down at the vial. This morning, it had felt like the most important thing in the world, a path to his salvation. Now it was just a lump of plastic.

The captain stood silent. Embarrassment pressed in on Clifford; he'd been so sure of himself, but his work was useless.

No. That wasn't true. If Tork was sure this was a waste

of time, that Clifford's knowledge wasn't worth the effort of saving him, then the captain would have walked away. Marel was always looking for a way to earn more, and for all of her calm, Tork came from the same place. The captain was using Clifford's desperation as leverage, a way to learn more. Clifford wasn't going to make it easy.

"This is worth ten times more," Clifford said. "At least. To make the serum we have now, you'd need to get materials past the blockade on an industrial scale, which is impossible. This is the first step to getting around it, to Valtech synthesising a solution to a disease no one else can cure. That's worth a fortune, to them and to you."

It felt absurd, reducing this thing to its financial value. Saving lives far outstripped such measures, as did the prestige it would bring, but these people were mercenaries and Clifford had to play to their values. Down here, he was a dead man, but Tork might be able to resurrect him.

"Didn't think you'd break quarantine," Tork said. "Why would a servant of the elders risk spreading disease to his earldom?"

Across the river, something like a deer sprinted along the bank. On this planet, every animal above the microscopic was good at one of two things, running or hiding. Without weapons to keep infected opponents at a distance, fighting back meant becoming swarm. Had Clifford become infected, not with the rot but with corporate values?

No. The Valtech team were a tool in a higher cause.

"The quarantine's been breached before, and it will be again," Clifford said. "If I can provide my people with a cure before that happens, then we'll beat death at its own game."

"You're not worried about transmission?"

"Your plan must have systems to counter the risk of infection, or your superiors wouldn't risk it."

"An isolated quarantine station when we enter orbit. Virtual contact with the corporation until we're deemed clean."

"I'll want more details before we go. I'm not risking anyone's lives on an ill-considered plan."

"Details are on a need-to-know basis."

"And if you want what I have, then you need me to know. Not about the extraction, keep that secret as long as you like, but about the steps that follow."

Tork stroked her chin and stared out across the water. There was something uncanny about her absolute calm. The stillness of the earldom's servants was a stillness that judged, in which small flickers of expression showed approval, dismissal, disgust. Tork had none of that. Weighing her own and her colleagues' lives in her hands, she remained still as the rocks beneath their feet.

"I'll need assurance," the captain said. "A written version of your findings, in case you don't survive extraction."

"If I write it down, you can take it and leave without me."

"Keep it on you—I'll only need it if you don't survive. This is going to be a rough ride."

"Very well."

"Then we have a deal."

Back home, they would have shaken on it. At Valtech, they would have signed a contract. Here, the deal was sealed in silence.

"Surprised you're keeping this from the Doc," Tork said. "Aren't you two close?"

Clifford's chest tightened. Acid clawed at his stomach, too long since he'd last eaten.

"Her faith sent her here to die," he said, hands curling around the blue vial. "I don't think she'd want to leave."

The river hissed by and the pipe gurgled. Solvesdin and Boran's voices rose from beyond Breda, the doctor's laughter comforting, the sergeant's a harsh snap. It was the warm laughter that burned Clifford.

"Emi believes in the blockade," he said. "She thinks that God created this place to challenge us, that we should live the best we can down here, not try to leave."

A bird circled overhead. Those with joints swollen by the rot couldn't rise above a low glide, but Clifford watched it nervously, just in case. He'd barely slept in weeks, too anxious for the shuffle of footsteps through the forest. Even safe in the belly of Breda's storage hold, wrapped in blankets and seclusion, he lay staring into the darkness, the certainty of destruction coming for him. He longed for just one quiet moment when he wasn't filled with the fear of death.

He knew that he was being selfish. He knew that he was being irresponsible. He knew that all his words were justifications. But he couldn't help himself: that gaping darkness, the unimaginable oblivion that came beyond death, scared him so much he could barely think.

"The Doctor wouldn't want to risk infecting other people," he said. "However good your containment plan is, she would say no. But I..."

He wanted to say that he had made a rational analysis based on everyone's best interests. The words stuck like stones in his throat.

"It's easy for the Doc." Tork's gaze bored into Clifford, delivering the truth he needed. "She's dying anyway. You're not. She's the one being selfish, if she won't share what we've learned here."

"Yes." Clifford nodded slowly. "Yes, you're right. Of course. We can't transmit what we know through the electronic blockade, so we have to leave."

"We do."

Tork's bracer beeped. With practised motions, she flicked a pill out of a dispenser on her belt, popped it into her mouth, and washed it down with water from a canteen. The Valtech logo on the canteen had been filled with red enamel.

"Was that Marel's?" Clifford asked, staring at the symbol on the canteen.

"You thought we'd ditch his stuff?"

"No, I..." He shouldn't say anything, but he couldn't help himself. "I'm sorry for your loss. It's not fair."

"He read the RBA."

"What's a—"

"Risk benefit analysis."

Tork spoke as if coming to Abaddon was just one more decision, like choosing what to eat for dinner, not the moment that had led Marel to his death. Clifford had seen people struggle with grief before. His mother's forced stillness when her father died, the darkness that hung over Aunt Prein after Aunt Vess' accident. You were allowed to let the sadness out at the funeral, to weep and wail and scream, to cry the well of tears dry, but then you had to move on. Had the captain been given a chance to do that?

"Did you bury him?" Clifford asked.

"Too risky with the rot."

"Then perhaps we could hold a memorial later, to remember him by?"

At last, a flicker of something crossed the captain's face, too fast for Clifford to comprehend. The pipe gurgled and sputtered, the tanks almost full.

"Sounds good," Tork said. "Something for when we get home."

"His family can join us."

"Exactly."

Clifford smiled and picked up the pipe, checking for how much water still flowed. Doing the right thing wasn't easy, but it was important. Tork and Boran would feel better once they said goodbye to their colleague.

"Doctor Solvesdin will be done soon," he said. "I should turn the pumps off and put this away. Will you let me know when the time for the extraction comes?"

"Of course." Tork gave a sharp nod, then turned away. "Good talking with you, Mister Foster."

Clifford checked that the tanks were full, then switched off the pump and reconnected Breda's solar panels to charge her main batteries. As he coiled the pipe, he paused to examine the dirt between the stones of the riverbank. It wasn't as rich as the soil in the forest, but something good could grow here.

"Hey, Cliff." Solvesdin appeared around the side of the truck, her medical bag slung over her shoulder. "Joom and Danna want to stick with us for the next few days, until the storm breaks and we can go gathering. What do you say, up for some company?"

It took Clifford a moment to process the names, to remember that the Valtech team had identities beyond Captain Tork and Sergeant Boran.

"That would be good," he said with a smile that almost felt natural.

"You OK?" She looked at him with concern, and he looked away.

"Just a stomach ache. Probably my body saying it's hungry." Solvesdin laughed.

"Always listen to your body, Cliff, or you'll end up having to listen to your Doctor." She stowed her bag then opened the door to Breda's main hold. "I'll find us some lunch."

Chapter Eight

Clifford sat in the dark in the back of Breda, patched blankets pulled up to his neck. For once, he was awake at night and not thinking about death. Instead, he was thinking about how well Doctor Solvesdin would be sleeping, lying in her reclining seat in the cab. Was she the sort of person who could sleep through anything, or the sort who came awake at the slightest sound in the night? It seemed strange that he hadn't worked that out by now. He wished that he'd paid more attention.

It wasn't like he could leave without her knowing. When a new day came and no one emerged from the hold, she would work out that he was gone. Perhaps, when she saw that the Valtech team were gone as well, she would realise what had happened. He hoped that she wouldn't be too upset, that she would understand why he'd had to do this. But whatever her response, sad or angry or accepting, he couldn't face her in the act. He hoped that she was a deep sleeper.

Beneath his blankets, the stopwatch on his belt buzzed, an alarm he hadn't needed. He pressed a button to stop it and discarded the blankets, then pulled a jacket on over his overalls, checked for the family photo in his pocket, picked up his testing kit, and eased the door open just enough to leave.

In the darkness of the night, he closed the door softly behind him.

Stars glared down as he walked across damp ground to the nearest of the giant trees. This storm had been a powerful one, the harvest afterwards large. He'd left the doctor with a good supply of ingredients, more than she would have gathered without him. In some ways, he was helping her, by not using up that supply.

"You look like you're going to a funeral, pup, not your fortune." A section of the tree peeled away, revealing itself as Boran. He stepped into a patch of moonlight and his bared teeth glowed bone white. "You got everything?"

Clifford held up the case. "Samples are here."

"And the notes?"

He patted a pouch tied to his belt.

"Come on then, cap's waiting."

The Valtech transport sat two trees over, its idling engine pulsing like a mechanical heart. Clifford had never been inside the vehicle before and it was everything he had expected, its constrictive bunks slotted between neatly arranged storage compartments, weapons and tools on shadow boards to mark where each one belonged. Compared with the make do and mend aesthetic of Breda, where every device and piece of furniture had been patched up or rewired, this place was reassuringly streamlined and new. Aside from the diamond logos on every object and door handle, the only decoration was a ball woven from strips of fur that hung above one of the bunks.

As soon as the door closed, the transport started moving. Its engine had none of Breda's rattle and roar. It was soft, smooth, a creature of well-oiled menace.

"Take a seat," Captain Tork said from the driver's seat.

"Twenty minutes to the evac site."

Boran slid into the bunk with the ball and folded his hands over his stomach, his bracelet of fangs lying pale against the fur of his wrist. Was it Clifford's imagination, or did those eyes stay open a crack, watching him? The urge to pace back and forth was so strong his thighs twitched, but he did as he was told, sitting on the hard floor near the back of the transport, his back against the wall. He took a bottle of sanitiser gel from his belt and cleaned his hands, checked the fastenings on his kit and his belt, cleaned his hands again. His foot tapped against the floor.

"Stop that," Boran growled.

"Sorry." Clifford clasped his hands in his lap. "What are you going to buy with your bonus?"

"Why?"

"It was something Marel talked about, so I was wondering, what are you going to buy?"

"Stocks. Bonds."

"You're investing it all?"

"Buying freedom, for later."

"I thought you corporate people were free already."

Boran's whiskers swayed in the gust of his snorted breath. The transport rolled on through the forest.

After a few minutes, the hiss of undergrowth against the vehicle's sides disappeared and the rumble of the wheels grew more intense. Clifford's heart beat faster. Were they running from swarm? That couldn't be right, Captain Tork would have called Boran up to snipe. They must just be out of the woods and speeding up to reach their extraction.

He licked his lips and leaned his head against the wall. The quiet curdled around him, so thick he felt he might choke.

"Have you served with Captain Tork for long?" he asked. Boran's disapproval was fierce, but this silent waiting was worse.

"Since the last Ossian War." Boran tapped the ball hanging over his bed, set it spinning on its axis like a miniature planet.

"That's a decade ago."

"And more."

"She must be a good commander."

"Yes."

Silence again, and the ball spinning in the gloom.

"Did you meet any of them? The Ossians, I mean?"

"The war was about them, not with them."

"It must be amazing, having the abilities they do. If you could remake a world, what would it be like?"

"Quiet."

Boran caught the ball, stopping its rotation. His claws stood out, straight and sharp, against its soft sides. Clifford, his mouth dry, slid further back into the corner.

As smoothly as it had accelerated, the transport eased to a stop.

"Everyone out," Tork said.

Clifford grabbed the handle of his test kit in a sweaty hand, opened the door with the other, and stepped out. Boran followed close behind, brushing against him as he passed. The short sword at the sergeant's waist, the rifle over his shoulder, and the point of his snout made his silhouette angular and unsettlingly inhuman against the deep grey of the star-strewn sky.

There was a brief spot of light in the darkness as Tork checked a screen on her bracer. She tipped her head back to watch the sky and Clifford, his eyes adjusting to the darkness, almost thought that he saw her smile.

"Do we have to set up a signal?" Clifford asked. "A light, a fire, a radio beacon perhaps."

"No signal," Tork replied. "We can't risk others in the blockade noticing. Everyone there has orders to shoot on sight."

"Then how will they find us?"

"This time and place were pre-arranged."

"What if they don't turn up?"

"Then we find our own way off, but that's not going to happen."

"It could. What if the others see the retrieval ship coming down, like they saw you? What if it's shot down like that raider ship? What if someone's too close and they don't even risk launching and—"

"Shut the fuck up," Boran hissed, the sound sending a shiver down Clifford's spine. When had the sergeant moved behind him?

Clifford didn't have to take that from Boran. A sergeant was equivalent in status to a junior researcher, and he could give him a piece of his mind. As the sole representative of the Earldom of Wecks he should, for the dignity of his people. Instead, he wrapped both arms around his sampling kit and stared up at the stars.

The minutes ticked by. One star moved across the black, and for a few minutes Clifford's hopes rose. He loosened his grip on the case. But the light kept moving away from them, just one more station in the orbital blockade. Insects chirped. Across the hills came a chittering noise, followed by a screech.

Was that an hour they'd been waiting? More? Clifford wanted to look at the time or to ask a question, but Tork's stillness and the silent presence of Boran behind his back held him in place. They waited, and so he waited.

There was something beautiful about the night sky, and terrible too. The light of stars shone from places and times unimaginably far away, while the darkness stretched on further past them than any living being could imagine. What was a human life compared with that? Clifford's life meant nothing by comparison, yet it was all he had.

He crouched, scooped up a handful of dirt, rubbed it between his fingers. It was hard to see the soil in the darkness, but it felt coarse, the sort of sandy soil that left the plains dry, home to withered grass and stunted bushes.

Tork touched her bracer. The glow from its small screen was just enough to sketch the outlines of her features, a ghostly skull against the blackness of night. The sight made Clifford take a step back. He'd never seen anyone so furious before.

Then the light went out and the captain spoke with her usual flat tone.

"They're not coming. One of the other stations must have spotted the launch and shot them down."

After seeing that expression on her face, the measured calm seemed so much darker, like spotting the shadow of a monster against the black of night.

"Are you sure?" Boran asked, his voice jagged as a splintered stump.

"We all knew the risks," the captain replied.

Clifford couldn't help wondering if they had. Valtech had promised its people an extraction, but was that ever a realistic option, with the blockade encircling the planet? Or were they scattered here like seeds across dead soil, in the hope that, against the odds, one would somehow find a way? How many lives would Valtech spend on a long shot, for a medicine that could change the universe?

Though the thoughts bubbled through Clifford's mind, he kept his mouth shut. He'd faced enough hopelessness of his own without spreading it to others.

Tork held out a canteen. "Water. Good to stay hydrated."

There was a hissing sound, so soft that Clifford almost didn't hear it. He turned to see Boran, one hand resting on the hilt of a long knife, his eyes black pits amid the moonlight grey of his fur.

The captain pushed the canteen into Clifford's hand, then opened the door of the transport. Clifford followed her in, then took his seat at the back of the transport, test kit in his lap. The water from the canteen was refreshing, but it couldn't wash away the bitterness of the night.

"You dropped this out there," Boran said as he climbed in, tossing something down on top of Clifford's test kit.

Clifford's eyes widened in alarm as he recognised his pouch of notes, the one he'd promised to bring along. This was everything that made him useful to these people. He couldn't afford to lose it.

"Thank you." He pressed the pouch against his chest. "I didn't even realise it was gone."

"Then pay attention," Boran snapped as he climbed into his bunk. He batted at the ball hanging over him, claws raking its fur, fangs rattling at his wrist. "But not now. Now, stop looking at me."

The engine purred into life, and they headed back the way they'd come.

*

Clifford didn't know how long he'd sat outside Breda, his back against one of the big wheels, before Solvesdin came out. Long enough for the sun to rise and the dawn chorus to sound. Long enough for strips of sunlight to shift across the soft dirt of the forest floor. Long enough for thoughts of death to become thoughts of home, stirred by the rich smell of healthy earth, then to cycle back to death again. Somewhere along the line, he took out the photo of his parents and tried to offer thanks for his life, but gratitude tasted like dust.

"Cliff?" Solvesdin looked down at him. "What are you doing out here?"

"Couldn't sleep." Like so many lies, it was a truth with its dark heart carved out. He put the photo away, leaving the other memento in his lap.

"What's that you've got there?"

"Canteen." Clifford held it up. "The Captain gave it to me."

"Huh." Solvesdin took the canteen and gazed at the red enamel embedded in its logo. "This was Marel's?"

"Yes."

"Good of Joom to give it to you."

Clifford shrugged. He wasn't so sure about that. Something else had passed in the darkness of the night, beyond the absence of a Valtech shuttle, something that left him unsettled and uncertain.

"Would you like to bury it?"

The unexpected question knocked Clifford's mind out of its slow, gloomy circles.

"Why would we do that?" he asked.

"We never gave poor Axio Marel a funeral."

"But we don't have a body."

"You don't need a body for a funeral. It's about the spirit."

Clifford sighed. "I don't believe in souls, Emi. Praying for Marel won't do him any good."

"Not for his spirit, for ours. None of us have many friends down here. How are we meant to move on if we don't take the time to grieve?"

"Tork and Boran have moved on well enough."

"I ain't so sure they have. We could invite them."

"Boran would laugh, and the Captain..."

The captain had given him this bottle for a reason, and he didn't think that it was to remember Private Marel.

"You're right, it would be mighty rude of us to ruin the Captain's phlegmatic poise."

Solvesdin held out a hand and Clifford let her help him to his feet. He didn't remember agreeing to the funeral, but it seemed that it was happening as Solvesdin took a spade from its housing on Breda's side and led him deeper into the woods.

"You pick a spot," she said. "Somewhere with good soil, where he'll easily find his way back to the cycle of life."

Beneath one of the giant trees was a smaller one that reminded Clifford of an apple tree on the farm back home, one he'd lain underneath when he was young, watching the ants at work and enjoying the play of sunlight on his skin. He brushed away the leaf mould and ran his fingers through the dirt, releasing a fragrance that was sweeter than it had been by Breda but still rich and comforting.

He held out his hand and Solvesdin handed him the spade. It was the good sort of worn; its wooden handle polished smooth by years of sweat and labour.

"There are up to fifty earthworms in a square foot of healthy soil," Clifford said, setting aside the first spadeful of dirt. "Thirty thousand species of micro-organisms in a single spoonful. Bacteria, fungi, nematodes, protozoa, a whole web of life. In the layer around the roots, you get exudates from a tree, the nutrients it releases into the soil, and all the life feeding off of that. I might not believe in God or souls or a wind carrying us to his will, but there's something miraculous about soil.

"This whole planet is teeming with life. The only ones who can't live here are us."

He stepped back and planted the spade, its bright blade biting into the dull brown of dirt. It felt good to dig, like his ancestors had done, to take control of one small patch of ground while the rest of his world spun out of control.

Solvesdin held out the canteen. "Would you like to say something?"

"You first. You're religious, you know how these things work."

"I suppose I do." A beam of sunlight caught the red diamond on the canteen's side. "Axio Marel could seem crude and thoughtless, but those are words we use to put down folks overflowing with life. In truth, he wanted the same things so many of us do, to enjoy the pleasures of this rich and wonderful universe. While his motives may not have been selfless, he died on a mission for a righteous cause, in search of medicine that would save others' lives. As the Book of Autumn says, 'the harvest need not match the seed for the store of my soul to be filled.'

"Axio's body has ceased its toil, but his presence lives on. As long as one memory of his smile remains with us, so does he. And so, we plant Axio in the earth from which we all come. His body may decay, but his spirit will endure."

She passed the canteen to Clifford.

The weight of the moment should have dragged him down. After all, this was a funeral, his last chance to say goodbye to a man who hadn't quite been a friend, but who he had needed in this place. Yet as he bowed his head over the canteen then lowered it into the hole, a crushing burden seemed to lift from his insides.

"It's no strip club with fancy drinks," he said, "but you wanted the finest things in life, and this is as good as Abaddon can provide. Thank you for sharing your dreams with us. They were shallow and stupid, but they were yours, and I'll miss you."

He plucked the spade from the earth and shovelled soil back in. The first few spadefuls clattered against plastic, then they became soft thuds, steady and reassuring. When the hole was full, he spread leaf litter over the top, to hide the scar in the earth. Solvesdin laid a spray of white blossoms on top.

"All cool?" she asked.

Clifford, leaning on his spade to stay upright, nodded.

"I don't think you are."

She wrapped her arms around him, and he sagged against her, the two of them clutching each other tight. Tears streamed down his face as sobs shook him. You were allowed to cry at funerals, even the absurd burial of a plastic bottle for a friend you barely knew. And though each sob was like a fever spasm, in the end he ached less rather than more.

Clifford straightened. Solvesdin was still leaning against him, eyes squeezed shut and lips pressed tight.

"Emi?" he asked. "Do you need more time?"

She shook her head. "The meds."

"You need more?"

She shook her head again. "They're the ones doing this. But it's that or..."

"Or face the void."

"Or return to the cycle of life, and right now, that doesn't sound any less scary."

Clifford slid an arm around her waist. He hoped that she didn't mind the dirt on his hand, but he hadn't had time to clean it.

"Here, take the spade for a walking stick, I'll help you back to Breda and then you can rest."

"When I die, find me a place like this," she said, shuffling her feet through the fallen leaves. "Somewhere beautiful where your micro-organisms can eat me."

"I will. I promise."

"Liar. You'll be off the planet by then."

His arm tightened around her. She knew. Not the details, perhaps, but the broad strokes. She wasn't angry or sad, didn't blame him. She accepted — the best and the worst thing she could do.

"No burial for your body, then," he said. "But I promise, your spirit will live on."

They took a more direct route back to Breda, without the wandering that had marked their search for a burial spot. Between the trees to the north, Clifford saw a distant hill, and a shape descending towards its peak. It was hard to tell at this distance, but it seemed too big for a bird.

Something rose out of the hill, like petals folding back from a flower. As the flying shape descended, sunlight glistened off a shiny surface. Something wet, or perhaps metallic, shaped a lot like a space shuttle. It disappeared from view and the ground folded back in.

"Did you see that?" Clifford asked.

"What, Cliff?" Solvesdin raised her head, but the thing was gone.

He hesitated, not wanting to give false hope, but in the end, it was impossible to ignore.

"It might be our way out."

Chapter Nine

Boran loped out of the bushes growing around the base of the hill. Moving at a crouch suited him, not quite on all fours but not a civilian stance, a pose made for the inevitability of attack. He jogged down into the low ground where they'd hidden the vehicles and saluted Tork.

"Foster was right," he said. "There's an opening on the south side, hidden in the turf, and a smaller one to the west. The scanner didn't pick up much metal or electrical activity, but that could be because it's buried. The whole place smells wrong." He wrinkled his snout, whiskers twitching, and looked at Clifford. "You think this is your people?"

Clifford shook his head. "No one told me about a base."

"No one told you about us either, pup." Boran turned his head and spat into the long grass.

"They would have let me know. It's important to my job."

"What about you?" Boran turned her gaze on Solvesdin. "Your people live in fucked up places."

"We don't hide; we just don't choose crowded environments. But I'm more concerned with what's in there than what ain't. We should think about why someone would be here before we act."

Tork leaned into the Valtech transport, took out a pair of backpacks, and handed one to Boran.

"What is that?" Solvesdin asked.

Tork held a laser pistol out to Clifford. There was red enamel in the diamond logo on its grip, the pistol that Marel had wanted to replace.

"You coming?" the captain asked.

Clifford took a deep breath then accepted the pistol. That shuttle was the closest he'd seen to a real chance for escape, and the Valtech team were still the people most likely to seize it. It seemed unlikely that someone hiding in a buried base would hand their transport over or play nicely with others who wanted their help.

"I've never shot a gun," he said, trying not to sound embarrassed.

"No recoil on a laser, just point and shoot."

"Joom, this is a mighty bad idea." Solvesdin called after Tork as she disappeared inside the transport. "We don't know who's in there or why. We should watch and wait, learn more before we act. Perhaps we can talk with them."

"No waiting." Tork emerged, a squat, hefty rifle in her hand. "Every day we're on this planet, more swarm close in. The only way out is to act fast and not stop until something works."

"Captain, please, think about what you're doing."

"I have."

"I'll come back once we've got the shuttle," Clifford said, looking down at his feet. The earth here was hidden by thick grass. "We can take you with us if you want, or at least say goodbye."

"To the wind with that." Solvesdin wrenched Breda's door open and pulled out her medical bag. "I'm not letting you fools die on your own."

They marched up the hill and around to the west, Boran leading the way. The grass grew shorter as they walked up slope and there were droppings from a small herbivore, the sort that Clifford's parents would have laid traps for to keep them from the crops. He shifted his grip on the pistol and wished that he'd taken shooting lessons when he had the chance, but this wasn't how his life was meant to go.

They stopped on a steeply sloped hillside where the grass grew thicker. Clifford pressed the green blades back and dug his fingertip into the dirt. Except that it wasn't dirt. Instead, there was a fibre mesh, interwoven with vein-thin feed pipes. Real plants growing on artificial ground.

Tork and Boran prodded at the ground with their combat knives, then took lumps of putty out of their bags and connected them with wires. At the captain's orders, everyone stepped away and lay flat, face down in the grass.

"Please, Joom," Solvesdin said. "There's still time to reconsider."

Tork tapped a button on her bracer. There was a thud, lower and softer than Clifford had expected, and the ground shook. Chunks of fake earth flew, and smoke billowed into the air.

"Go, go, go!"

Tork and Boran were on their feet, rifles in hands, dashing through the smoke. Clifford ran after them and Solvesdin followed.

The explosives had blown a hole three metres across in the grass and fake ground beneath, torn ends of mesh peeling back around the edges, dark liquid seeping from them. Beneath was a pale surface, charred by the explosives. In the centre, a door had fallen in, revealing a tunnel into the hillside.

The smoke was flowing outward, carried by a steady current of air. Lights embedded in the bone pale ceiling illuminated the shapes of Tork and Boran, their clothing no camouflage in the tunnel, as they stalked slowly into that stark world.

With a spitting sound, soft projectiles burst like blisters against the wall next to Boran. He flung himself to the ground, even as their spatter hissed on his sleeve. Tork fired, two shots in swift succession, and in the confines of the tunnel it sounded like the earth breaking. Down the corridor, something shattered, pink ooze spraying back across the ceiling. The spitting sound stopped.

Back on his feet, Boran advanced down the tunnel, the barrel of his rifle swaying purposefully. He paused, aiming ahead, and Tork passed him, then took her turn to wait, the two of them alternating advances into the hill.

Clifford wanted to be part of their progress, to contribute something to their work. But he didn't trust himself to spot the dangers they would, or to protect either of them if a threat came. More than anything else, he didn't want to be the one charging into the unknown, to face whatever threats the hill held. Cowardly as it was, he hung back with Solvesdin in the tunnel mouth, clutching Marel's pistol just in case.

Suddenly, a section of the wall shot out, slamming into Tork. Something moved and Boran fired into the gap, his longer rifle speaking muted fury. Glistening red tubes flopped into the tunnel, the detached wall fell with a crack, and silence descended.

Boran looked at Tork, who was picking herself up off the floor. She shook her head, then started advancing again.

Cautiously, still keeping his distance, Clifford followed them, and Solvesdin followed him.

"Clear," Boran called from a doorway, then swivelled to aim down the tunnel.

"Clear," Tork called from the next doorway down.

Clifford paused where the section of wall had detached. The red mess on the floor didn't look like anything mechanical, but like the waste from an abattoir. He squeezed his mouth tightly shut, suppressing the humiliating urge to vomit.

As he forced himself to step over that mess, a smaller gap opened in the ceiling between him and the Valtech team.

"Behind you!" he shouted, flinging himself to the ground.

There was a spitting sound, the spatter and hiss of acid projectiles, then the twin bellows of Tork and Boran's guns speaking in unison. The spitting stopped.

Clifford looked up. Tork and Boran were already moving on, though the sergeant now looked back every few steps. It was only as his gaze passed over him that Clifford remembered the pistol in his hand. His cheeks burned.

At the end of the tunnel was a door made from the same pale substance as the walls. Tork fired her rifle at the control pad next to the door. Instead of electrical sparks, pink liquid oozed from the broken pad. Boran rammed his claws into the edge of the door and strained. There was a scraping sound, a crackling and popping as something gave way, and the door slid into the wall.

Tork stepped through.

"Stop right there," she said and fired a single shot, the weapon's crack echoing down the tunnel. "Hands in the air."

"It's all right," a fluting voice said. "I am completely unarmed.

"Hands. Now."

When they'd been chased by the swarm, Clifford had been afraid. Franticly, heart-racingly afraid, knowing that something terrible was coming after him. But at least he had known what he was facing, and no matter how bad things had got, some animal part of him had felt that if he just ran far enough and fast enough, he could be safe. This was different. He didn't know what he was facing or why. Even the walls were strange, their surface not quite smooth to the touch, like a white and shiny concrete.

He stepped through the doorway into a room the size of a farm kitchen. Rows of glass jars filled shelves on two of the walls, each one neatly labelled. Against the third wall was a workbench with a bright light above. Lumps of flesh sat on it, some with nodules protruding along their edges, one with bone stems sticking out the top.

Standing by the bench with her hands in the air was the strangest woman that Clifford had ever seen. She was over six feet tall, stick thin, a sleeveless blue robe falling down her body in shimmering folds. Gold jewellery dotted with shining gems lay against skin so white it was almost translucent. Her skin was peeling in places, especially around her night black eyes, which were twice as large as they should be, and around the bony lumps that protruded from her forehead and arms. For a moment, he wondered if she had chalk rot, but there were no dark veins through the paleness, no crumbling flesh.

"Where's the shuttle?" Tork asked.

"You could introduce yourselves," the woman said. "If you're going to barge into—"

The butt of Tork's rifle slammed her back against the workbench.

"Where?" Tork snapped.

"Through that door, third right, but you can't open the bay without me."

"Bet that's what you thought about the door." Boran sniggered.

"How many others are here?" Tork asked, twisting the woman around.

"Just me." The woman winced as her hands were bound behind her back with a cable tie.

"Security systems?"

"You're past them."

Tork pushed her to the ground by her workbench then bound her ankles with swift, efficient movements.

"Boran, with me. Foster, guard her. Don't let her move."

"I..." Clifford swallowed. Breaking in had made sense, but holding this woman at gunpoint felt wrong.

"Problem?" Tork asked.

"No, it's fine." Clifford shook his head. What else was he going to do? And what harm was there in guarding her when she was already bound? Once Tork came back, they could talk this through.

Boran wrenched another door open, and the two soldiers strode out of the room.

"Are you OK?" Doctor Solvesdin knelt beside the woman and drew a scanner from her bag.

"A little ruffled."

"My name's Doctor Emieke Solvesdin, but you can call me Emi."

"Desilian Vang. I would say that it's a pleasure to meet you, but that would feel disingenuous in the circumstances."

"These protrusions, they're part of you?"

"I'm not sick, if that's what you're asking. But given the noise you made coming in here, I expect that swarm will be descending soon, and then everybody's prognosis takes a turn for the worse."

Alarmed, Clifford looked back down the entrance tunnel, but there was no sign of movement. Tork's plan made sense as long as they got in the shuttle and got out fast, but if they didn't, if swarm responded to the disturbance, if the presence of untainted bodies excited them as it often seemed to do...

"Shouldn't you be pointing that gun at me?" Vang asked, looking at Clifford.

Solvesdin's head jerked around, and she glared at him. "Well?"

"I don't really want to, but..."

"But you're worried about your friends." Vang blinked her huge black eyes, the lizard-like gesture sending a shiver through Clifford. "I quite understand."

"Cliff, put the gun down," Solvesdin said. "You're too good a man for this nonsense."

He hesitated, then thrust the gun through his belt. The jars on the wall had caught his eye again. Some of them contained insects and plants, others samples of earth. Labels included the coordinates at which they had been collected, locations all across Abaddon.

"What are you doing here?" he asked.

"Studying. Cataloguing. Recording what my people left behind."

"Your people?"

Vang dipped her head, drawing attention to the bony growths. By her feet, Solvesdin had brought out a knife and was cutting through the cable tie. Clifford tensed. Tork would want him to stop her releasing Vang.

"You're Ossian," he said, putting together fragments from news reports, rumours, and childhood stories. "The terraformers."

"I am."

"Your people made Abaddon?" A sick feeling settled in him. He wasn't so sure that he wanted to see her released any more. "You made the chalk rot?"

"Not on purpose." Her hands released, Vang rose to her feet. "But rebuilding the reality of a planet is a hazardous business." She stroked one of the extrusions on her forearm. "Things never go entirely to plan, and our techniques were cruder in those days."

"You've been here ever since?"

She laughed and pushed strands of grey hair back behind her ear. "I'm old, but not millennia old."

Clifford blushed and looked back at the jars.

"I didn't mean to be rude." His hand settled on the pistol. "I'm just trying to understand."

"Then we share something in common. I came here to try to understand a past mistake and perhaps to make up for it. I knew that I wouldn't be able to leave, but that was fine. My people did this, the least we can do is to undo it."

"You made the serum, didn't you?"

"I did. Then I spent the next year teaching every survivor I could find. But even with it, they didn't last long. I gave up on trying to build a society here. Perhaps I didn't deserve the company."

"Quit the self-pity," Solvesdin said. "Why didn't you transmit your findings up to orbit? If you could get safely through the blockade, you must have something that can penetrate the communications field."

Vang's finger ran across her protrusions again as she gazed at the rows of samples.

"You're making big assumptions about my capabilities, Doctor Solvesdin, and I'm afraid that I may not live up to your expectations. I did try to transmit my results, or at least the fact of their existence, but I did not receive a fruitful response. I did see an increase in armed expeditions, if that helps."

Clifford's hand tightened around the grip of the pistol.

"That's why the corporations keep sending them," he said. "They're not just trying to find out if there's a cure, they know there is."

"But you didn't know about it?" Vang raised a slender eyebrow. "Interesting. Why is that?"

"The quarantine blockade. They don't let anyone leave in case they carry an infection."

"I wasn't trying to leave."

"No transmissions either, in case someone tries to coordinate a way around the blockade."

"Does that really make sense, given the threat this planet represents?"

"Yes, of course."

Clifford frowned. He'd read the documents, he'd listened to the briefing, but it was only now, at the heart of it all, that he questioned the bigger picture. Surely there was a way to get the medicine safely out?

Solvesdin took a deep, ragged breath and clutched her side.

"Emi." Clifford hurried to her. "Are you all right?"

"Stupid meds," she hissed between gritted teeth. Her skin was turning a yellower shade of green. She leaned against the wall, and as her head slumped her hat fell.

"It's all right," Clifford said, easing her to the floor. "We're almost done here. You can rest on the shuttle, or back at Breda."

"Breda." Solvesdin smiled. "You can have her when I'm gone. That would be cool."

"You're not going anywhere."

Her laughter turned into a cough, which she stifled, then gave him a rueful grin.

"Neither are you, Cliff. Don't you get that yet?"

Chapter Ten

Clifford peered out of the door and down the tunnel. A patch of blue sky was distantly visible at the far end. Was it his imagination or was something moving there? He clutched the pistol tight, its grip hard in his hand, and wiped the sweat from his brow.

"Fuck, pup, but you're a useless guard."

Clifford spun around to see Boran standing in the other doorway. His rifle wasn't pointing at the unbound Vang, but it was close.

Shifting from foot to foot, Clifford drew in against the door frame.

"Sorry," he said, "I just—"

"The Cap wants her. Come on, all of you."

"I'd rather not," Vang said, her high voice steady.

Boran's rifle was quieter than Tork's, but the shattering of a shelf and all the jars on it made Clifford jump.

"You overestimate my attachment to my own survival," Vang said with an icy smile.

"How fucking noble of you."

Boran grabbed the Ossian woman and dragged her across the room. With a sigh, Vang let herself be led out. Clifford and Solvesdin followed.

The corridors of the base continued as they had before, and so did the Valtech team's approach to moving through them. Two more doorways hung open, their control panels bleeding pink ooze down the walls, the damage made more unsettling by the traces of veins beneath the surface and the marks like freckles around doorways.

"Did you grow this place?" Clifford asked, trying to hide his incredulity.

"Me?" Vang asked. "No."

"But someone did?"

"That's a complicated question."

"Complicated how? Either this place was grown, or it was built."

Vang chuckled. "As you grow older, you'll learn that life isn't as clearly bounded as you think."

Her tone rankled. He wanted to tell her that he wasn't a child, that he was quite capable of coping with ambiguity, that refusing to provide information wasn't the sign of wisdom she seemed to think it was. But someone who ran a place like this was surely his superior, so he should listen and show respect.

They stepped through another broken doorway into a chamber whose ceiling was a tilting dome made from rubbery, overlapping layers. In the centre of the room sat a bulbous shape like a twenty-foot maggot, one end pointed and the other flared open, with chitinous wings folded back against its flanks. Tork stood by its side, the body of her rifle dark against that pale, fleshy shape.

"This the shuttle you saw?" she asked.

Clifford stared, trying to make sense of what he was looking at. "It could have been."

"You got any other transport?"

Vang shook her head. "I had to bring something small to slip past the blockade unnoticed. It's quite sufficient for travelling around the planet."

"Could it get back to orbit?"

"In theory, yes. But do you really think that you'll get through the blockade?"

"Open it."

"I don't think that's a good idea."

Boran's hand whipped through the air, claws ripping through Vang's upper arm. Blood spattered the white wall. Vang shrieked and clapped a hand onto the wound, more blood running between her pale fingers. Her expression was pure indignation.

"Open it or there's more like that," Boran hissed.

"If death is the price I must pay to keep the disease here, then I will pay it."

"It won't be death." Boran stepped to within an inch of Vang, looking up into the pale woman's face. He pressed his claws against Vang's neck and took a deep breath, like he was smelling her fear. "It'll be pain. Slow, drawn out pain, clawing strips of flesh away until there's nothing but raw, bloody nerves."

Clifford stared, aghast. He had known that he was working with soldiers, but he'd always assumed that they lived by some sort of code.

"I'm not afraid to face the consequences," Vang said, closing her eyes. "To pay the price for what we did here."

"I ate a man on the Yistral campaign. Good for him that he was dead first, but it didn't have to be that way." Boran leaned into Vang's injured arm and ran a long tongue across bloodstained fingers. "I've been wondering what an Ossian would taste like, one piece at a time."

The pistol shook in Clifford's hand. This wasn't right, and he wanted to raise the gun in protest. But in a fight between them, Boran would kill him as easily as breathing.

He looked at the shuttle. They were almost out of this terrible place. He just had to hold on a little longer.

"Fine." Vang gave a trembling nod. "I'll do it."

"Good girl."

As Boran led Vang to the shuttle, Tork turned to Clifford.

"Do you have your test kit?" the captain asked.

"It's on Breda."

Tork frowned. "Your notes?"

"Right here." Clifford patted a pouch attached to his tool belt.

"Throw it to me." Tork held out her hand.

"Why?"

"Why do you think?" Tork pointed her rifle at Clifford. The movement was so easy, so casual, it took a moment for its menace to sink in.

Next to Tork, Vang and Boran climbed up the shuttle's wing, approaching a muscle-like disk in its side.

"But why?" Clifford asked. "We can all leave."

"To share what you've learned with the universe?" Tork snorted. "I almost feel sorry for you, Foster."

"We can cure the chalk rot, end the blockade and the risk of an outbreak. Isn't that why we're all here?"

"I'm here to make a profit, and you're holding it. Now throw me the notes."

The rifle pointed at Clifford and the void opened beneath him, but he didn't have to accept that end. He didn't have to give up his work or the life it came with.

He pointed the laser pistol at Tork, fighting hard to keep it steady, to keep his fear from showing.

"No recoil on a laser," Clifford croaked. "Just point and shoot, right?"

"No battery in that laser," Tork replied.

Clifford hesitated. Surely that was a lie? They'd been working together, Tork wouldn't have given him a useless weapon with the swarm outside and unknown threats inside.

The rifle kept pointing at him, its mouth an invitation to the darkness he felt within.

Clifford pulled the laser pistol's trigger. There was a faint click.

"You lied," he whispered.

"Of course," Tork said. "We want what everyone in the blockade wants: to stop others getting through. You think your station was destroyed by accident? Every ship and station has standing orders to shoot anything coming off the surface. You sent drones down for soil samples, and that was the end."

"The samples didn't come to our station. There was no risk of infection."

"You were told to work in secret, right? That other people might misunderstand? But they understood. If we get through, then Valtech will make a fortune selling new medicines to your elders, and that doesn't work if you share the secrets." Tork's face was so still, her voice so flat, she could have been describing the weather, not the thinking that led to someone else's death. "Our odds of success aren't good, but the bonus will buy me a longer, healthier life than anyone I've ever met. So, throw me your notes, or I'll blow your brains out."

Clifford dropped the useless pistol and, with trembling fingers, unfastened the pouch from his belt. What was the point of resisting? Even his own people cared so little that they'd put him in the firing line. One more young life thrown away to preserve the wisdom of the elders. He had been a dead man before he even reached the planet; at least down here he knew.

The wet sound of the shuttle door opening made Clifford flinch. He threw the pouch to Tork, who caught it one-handed. The rifle never wavered in its aim.

"Smart lad," Tork said. "Enjoy your last few days down here."

"What the fuck is this?" Boran asked as he stared inside the shuttle. "How are we meant to fit in there?"

"It was all I needed," Vang said. "Smaller was better for slipping through the blockade."

"What about supplies?"

"They were here already."

Boran spat over the side of the wing, then straightened as he turned to face Tork. His rifle was slung over his shoulder and his hand rested casually on the pommel of his short sword.

"Space for one?" Tork asked.

"Yes, Cap."

"Oh."

Tork turned. Boran leaped. Her rifle barked. His head exploded, spattering blood and worse across Vang, who screamed. With a wet thud, Boran's body hit the floor, his sword clanging down beside him.

Clifford sank to his knees, bile burning his throat. He stared at the blood streaming from where Boran's head had been, soaking into his fur, reddening the pale fangs around his wrist, spreading across the floor in a dark pool. Then he looked up, his eyes drawn to Tork's rifle. Would it point at him next? At Solvesdin? Would the crack of its firing be the last sound he ever heard?

Tork looked down at the body.

"Sorry, Sergeant," she said, and she could almost have meant it.

Rifle at the ready, Tork climbed up the wing and stood over Vang, who leaned against the pale side of the shuttle, her black eyes bulging.

"How intuitive is this thing to fly?" Tork asked. When Vang didn't respond, she slapped her with the pouch. "Do you really want to die?"

Vang stared at the body. Just like Clifford, she was shaking from head to toe.

"Purple," she blurted out. "Purple tendrils running from the ceiling. Connect them to your temples. The shuttle will interpret your commands."

Tork shoved her off the wing, into the blood below, then climbed into the shuttle. Its door closed. The wings unfolded and there was a humming as the engines started up.

Solvesdin hauled Clifford to his feet. Her hands were shaking, face crumpled in pain and frustration.

"Come on," she said. "We should get out of here."

"I'm sorry," he said, still staring at the corpse. That would be him, soon enough. "I thought we could get out. I thought that..."

"No time." Solvesdin hurried over to Vang, who was kneeling in Boran's blood, staring at the red stains on her hands. "You too, come on."

Solvesdin grabbed Vang's bony arm.

The ground trembled. Above their heads, the pink layers of the ceiling peeled back, revealing the blue of the sky. A bird gliding on a low wind let out an unsettling screech. Its wings were tattered, clumps of feathers missing, the remainder covered in white dust.

The shuttle rose, taking Clifford's last hope of escape. Air blasted out beneath the ship, carrying a scent of rot. The bird screeched again, and distant creatures called back.

"We have to go," Solvesdin headed for the door, dragging Clifford and Vang with her.

With a throbbing rumble of hidden engines, the shuttle passed the opening.

"Let go of me!" Clifford wrenched his arm free. "I'm done running, done hiding, done barely surviving. There's no escape. We're dead either way."

He slapped a hand over his mouth. Solvesdin was a doctor. She was more qualified, more experienced, more respected than him. He mustn't talk to a doctor like that.

The absurdity of it hit him like the down draft from the shuttle's engines, almost knocking him off his feet. A laugh erupted from inside, ridiculous and powerful, its rough edges ripping through his chest. His lips peeled back in a terrible rictus as he let the sound shake him.

Who cared about status when they were all dead?

Somehow, he wasn't surprised to see Solvesdin smile back.

"If you're done barely surviving," she said, "what are you going to do instead?"

Chapter Eleven

Clifford emerged from the hole in the hillside, Solvesdin and Vang to either side of him. The smoke was gone, but the air still smelled of soot, and a little like charred flesh.

There was blood on Vang's arms, on her face, in her hair, but none on her clothes. Every drop slid straight off the shimmering fabric, so that it looked as though her clothing were drawn from a different world. There was blood on Solvesdin too. Not just blood. Boran. One more life snuffed out. One more absence that, for better or for worse, could never be repaired.

The shuttle was overhead, becoming smaller with every moment. The wings were visible, but the organic texture of its hull could have been mistaken for plastic or paint. The sound of its engines and the wind of its passage swept over the forest, shaking the treetops and startling birds into the air.

The swarm had heard the engines. Scores of them, hundreds even, had emerged from the tree line, whether drawn by the shuttle, the sounds of conflict within the hill, or perhaps the scent of living prey. Some of them looked up with dead, bulging eyes, watching Tork's escape. Others were moving toward the hill, picking up speed as they went.

At this distance, Clifford could just make out the edge of the low ground where they'd hidden Breda, halfway to the tree line and the monsters it held. In that moment, the dip in the ground looked dangerously far away.

There was no point going back into the hill with a hole blown open in its side and there was no way they could stay ahead of the swarm on foot. Part of him, smelling smoke and staring at the trees, was flung back to his first day on Abaddon, to the certainty that his life was over. That part of him wanted to give in, to accept that he was disposable, the way that Tork saw him. The way the Earldom did. But that part wasn't in charge.

He didn't even make the choice to run. His legs propelled him across the open ground, arms swinging, heart racing, breaths coming fast. The swarm ran to meet him, a chittering, screeching mass of bodies, warped by the chalk rot. Solvesdin and Vang fell behind, unable to match Clifford's speed.

The shuttle was shrinking as it soared toward the upper atmosphere. Then there was a flash, something streaking across the sky, and an explosion, a flower of fire blooming where the shuttle had been.

No one got out of Abaddon alive.

Clifford sprinted toward the dip in the ground, slid down the slope, slammed into one of Breda's wheels. A creature came over the rise, wolf-like body swollen around the shoulders, its bald muzzle pale and striped with jagged veins. Clifford yanked a door open, leaped in, slammed it shut just before the creature reached him, snapping and scratching at the metal. He climbed into the driver's seat, Solvesdin's seat, while the thing hissed and growled and scratched.

More swarm poured down the slope toward him. One, its body a terrible distortion of humanity, leaped onto the bonnet and hammered at the windscreen.

A tin fell from the dashboard, scattering fried insects around his feet, as Clifford fumbled with the controls. He started the engine and slammed his foot down. Breda roared out of her hiding place, up toward the hill. He jerked the wheel and the creature on the bonnet went flying. It was dead already, he told the part of himself that felt guilty at killing, but he had a chance to live.

More swarm were running toward Solvesdin and Vang, fast moving creatures on all fours. Clifford drove toward them, through them, over them, scattering and crushing twisted bodies. His teeth were gritted, his heart pounding, but he held the wheel steady, kept his foot on the accelerator until he was almost at the others. Then he hit the brakes and swung Breda around, between the survivors and the swarm.

He flung the door open. Solvesdin and Vang scrambled in. Something snapped at their heels, catching the edge of Vang's robes. She kicked and it fell, a strip of shimmering fabric between its teeth. Before Solvesdin could shut the door, Clifford hit the accelerator again.

All around them, warped bodies emerged from between the huge trees, chunks of rotten flesh falling away in dust as they ran, death streaming from beneath the beautiful green canopy. With nowhere to go, no storm to chase, Clifford picked a marker to steer by, a sign in the sky like the stars used by navigators of old: the cloud of smoke and falling debris that had been the shuttle.

That shuttle had been their chance to get something off the planet, to reach out and touch the universe again. If he couldn't escape, then at least his learning might have done, if not for a missile streaking out of the blockade like the vengeance of an angry god.

Except that the dream had never been real. Abaddon was the land of the dead, and there was no coming back.

"Goodbye," Clifford said to the smoke that had been Captain Tork. Then Breda reached the forest's edge, and that guiding sight disappeared between the leaves.

*

They didn't have bodies or even possessions to remember Joom Tork and Danna Boran by. Instead, they painted Valtech diamonds on a pair of stones by the riverbank, set in thick mud that would swallow them in time, just like it swallowed the remains of Abaddon's past.

"I don't understand," Vang said. She stood back from Clifford and Solvesdin, her bandaged arm in a sling. "They were violent thugs who threatened us all. They don't deserve remembrance."

"Funerals aren't just for the dead," Clifford said. "They're for the living."

Solvesdin squeezed his hand. "That was mighty well said."

He slid his arm around her shoulders and hugged her tight. This wasn't something friends did back home: too informal, too embarrassingly intimate. But those people back home hadn't been through what he had.

He took the photo from his pocket and smiled sadly down at the image of his parents, taken in front of the farmhouse. Their smiles were so bright, that was how he liked to think of them, but by now there would have been tears. Friends and family gathering together for a moment like this one, a ceremony without a body in the orchard where they laid farm folks to rest. A single stone with his name carved into it. They would weep, and then they would put death behind them, to get on with life.

Clifford was alive and he was dead; the one had always been running toward the other.

For better or for worse, the Valtech team would live on. After all, they'd changed him, and that would keep him alive. In a few days, when he went back for their transport and the supplies inside the hill, the memories of them would be all around, ghosts in the places where they had walked, stains on the ground where Boran had died. He thought of the fur ball hanging over the sergeant's bunk, a child's toy in a vehicle built for war, and for a moment his breath was too heavy to take.

"You could bury me beneath one of the big trees," Solvesdin said. "I'd like part of me to reach that high again."

You weren't meant to talk about death, because that invited it in. Clifford had never appreciated how much harder that made everything.

"That sounds beautiful," he said. "Anything else?"

Solvesdin looked up at him and laughed. "I thought you'd try to change topic."

"We're dead people waiting for the end." He pointed to the blue expanse that hid the blockade above and the universe beyond it. "Just like everyone else."

The void was there, when he thought about these things. The certainty that, in the end, he would be nothing. It was the most terrifying feeling in a world full of death and pain. But he didn't try to push the thought aside or let himself sink into it. Instead, he gathered his thoughts around it: how long he might have, what he could do with that time, how he might live on when his body joined Solvesdin's underneath that tree. If he held those thoughts close to the void, then he didn't have to face it alone, and his hopes shone brighter against the dark.

"Since I got here, we've spent our whole time running from the swarm," he said. "What if we run towards something instead?"

"Go on."

"With what I've learned, we can make the serum faster and build up spare supplies. We can look for other survivors instead of running into them. We can build a community."

"The minute you settle down, the swarm will find you." Vang pointed to the foundations of a long gone building jutting like broken bones through the flesh of the far riverbank. "There's no escaping what my people made here."

"So, we make a community that keeps moving, one that scatters and comes back together, sharing expertise and supplies. We'll experiment with the serum, maybe find a real cure or a way to kill the swarm. We'll make this a world where people live, not just survive."

"You can't beat death."

"That's why I'm not going to fight it, or to keep running from it, as if that's all there was in the world." He picked up the test kit sitting by his feet. A twisted shape was approaching out of the distance, some beast of burden with its fur fallen out and half the flesh gone from its skull. It moved slowly for now, but it would soon move faster. "I should take samples before we leave."

While Solvesdin got Breda ready, Clifford knelt in the mud. He sank his fingers through the rich, damp dirt, caught the scents of clay, silt and decaying weeds. Maybe they could plant seeds in places like this and return to gather food another year. Perhaps they could leave stashes of medicine and directions to meeting places, lifelines for others to find. Perhaps just pictures and poems, reminders of what it meant to be alive.

Birds sang, the river adding its soft sound to their trilling chorus. A fish burst from the current, caught a fly, disappeared into the water again. A familiar, rat-like creature poked its head out of a gap between the roots of a riverside tree, and Clifford waved hello.

A dead man filled three small pots with dirt, put them into the case his aunt had given him, and walked back to the truck, smiling as he went.

Discover Luna Novella in our store:

https://www.lunapresspublishing.com/shop